TWO DOGS IN A TRENCH COAT

Start a Club by Accident

TWO DOGS IN A TRENCH COAT

Start a Club by Accident

by Julie Falatko

Illustrated by Colin Jack

Scholastic Press / New York

Library of Congress Cataloging-in-Publication Data available

ISBN 978-1-338-18953-7

10 9 8 7 6 5 4 3 2 1   19 20 21 22 23

Printed in the U.S.A.   23
First edition, February 2019

Book design by Elizabeth Parisi

For Lindsay and her excellent and
abundant knowledge of floats

CHAPTER ONE

Thee is the bell," Waldo said to Sassy. "Time to go home and dig a hole in the backyard for no reason."

"I can't wait to nap," said Sassy.

Then Sassy stretched, and Waldo almost fell off her. He'd gotten used to this. He spent weekdays balancing on top of her, wrapped in a trench coat.

"One day we will go to the ocean," Waldo said. "And I will be a top-notch, number one, **meatball**-winning surfing champion, thanks to all this practice I get surfing on top of you while you stand up and lie down with no regard to the fact that I am up here."

"If you win **meatballs**, you better share," said Sassy.

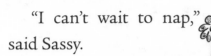

Waldo spent the day balancing on top of Sassy, wrapped in a trench coat, because on school days they pretended to be a human student. It was an excellent disguise. Everyone thought they were a human student named Salty, who had come to Bea Arthur Memorial Elementary School and Learning Commons from the town of Liver, Ohio. Really though, they just wanted to make sure their boy, Stewart, wasn't being tormented by an evil, giant, hairy monster every day at the mysterious place called school. He wasn't. But then

the dogs discovered that they loved school. They loved having grown-ups give them jobs, and then completing those jobs. They loved running fast in gym and singing songs in music. And most of all they loved the cafeteria. On the weekends, they got bowls of dry **kibble** twice a day. But on weekdays, they got those bowls of **kibble** *and* they got school lunch, which was always the most delicious food imaginable.

So now the dogs went to school, and sat at the desk next to Stewart in Ms. Twohey's class, and made friends, and took spelling tests, and ate lunch every day.

And while they loved school very much, they also loved going home at the end of the day to run in circles in the backyard, make sure no squirrels got into the house, and then nap for three hours.

"Goodbye, MS. Twohey," said Waldo. "Thank you for the best Monday. I love Monday!"

"Oh, you," said Ms. Twohey. "Good work painting that giant R for the Founders Day banner."

"That is the first time I have ever painted a giant letter, which proves you are the best teacher."

The dogs caught up with Stewart in the hall.

"Time for our nap!" said Sassy from underneath the trench coat.

"You nap all afternoon under the desk," said Waldo.

"Napping makes me want to nap."

"You can go on home without me," said Stewart. "I have a Junior Office Supply Enthusiasts meeting."

"What?" said Waldo.

"You want us to just . . . go home? By ourselves?" asked Sassy.

"Sure," said Stewart. "You know the way."

"That's not how we do it," said Waldo. "You always walk home with us."

"Well, yes," said Stewart. "I know. But my parents told me I had to join a club, because it will look good on my college applications."

"What are **cauliflower apple tasters**?" asked Waldo.

"Don't worry about it. They found out that the school has a branch of this club they both loved when they were kids, and they told me I should start thinking about my future."

"Sure," said Sassy. "Like how sometimes I think about lunch while I'm eating breakfast. It's good to plan."

"We will come to the meeting with you!" said Waldo. "Will there be snacks? I smell snacks. And **old meat**. Will there be **old meat** snacks?"

"I don't know," said Stewart. "Maybe. Mostly it's about sticky notes and paper clips."

"I have another question," said Waldo. "A club is a kind of **sandwich**, right? How do you join a **sandwich**?"

"A club can also be a group of people—" said Stewart.

"Or dogs," said Sassy.

"Or dogs," said Stewart. "A group of people or dogs who have a common interest and meet to talk about it. And no, not that kind of '**meat**.'"

"I have another question," said Waldo.

"Yes?"

"Is there a **club sandwich** club?"

"I don't think so."

"There should be," said Sassy.

"I would join a **club sandwich** club," said Waldo.

"Then we could **meat**," said Sassy.

Stewart looked at the clock on the wall. "I have to go. We can talk more about clubs and **sandwiches** later."

"Something smells delicious," said Waldo. "We will go with you to your **club sandwich**."

"Are you sure?" said Stewart.

Waldo's eyes got very sad. "You do not want us there."

"What? Of course I want you there," said Stewart. "I just thought you wanted to go home and nap."

"I want that!" said Sassy from under the trench coat. "But we will not leave you."

"Every activity that's a Stewart activity is the best activity!" said Waldo.

"You're our boy!" agreed Sassy.

CHAPTER TWO

Stewart and Salty walked to the second grade class-room where Junior Office Supply Enthusiasts was meeting.

"Hello, and welcome!" said the teacher in the room, who was lining pencils up in neat rows on a table. "I'm Mr. Nehi, and I'm here to guide you on your journey through the most passionate and rewarding hobby I know: the love of office supplies!"

"I'm Stewart."

"I'm Salty. I am from Liver, Ohio," said Waldo. "Where are the snacks?"

"Maybe there will be snacks later," said Mr. Nehi.

"Ha ha ha!" said Waldo.

"What's so funny?" asked Mr. Nehi.

"I thought you were making a human joke," said Waldo. "Because there are always snacks later. I am most interested in snacks right now."

"I never joke about office supplies," said Mr. Nehi. "Now, let's get started. Today we'll introduce ourselves and talk about our relationships with office supplies. If anyone has a meaningful anecdote about office supplies, you may share it. Then we'll do some deep diving into highlighters, some important sticky-note work, and then, *if we have time*, we'll have a snack."

"Excuse me, Mr. Office Supplies, I need to discuss something important with Stewart right now in the hallway," said Waldo.

"Is it about office supplies?" asked Mr. Nehi.

"Oh yes, definitely," said Waldo.

"Okay, but be quick."

Stewart followed Salty into the hallway. "What is it?"

"We cannot stay in your pencil club."

"Why not?"

"There is no snack," said Waldo.

"We have no **meatball** antidote about office supplies," said Sassy. "Also it is very, very boring."

"And we cannot be in a club where a snack is a sometimes maybe activity," said Waldo.

Stewart sighed. "Yeah, that's okay. I didn't think you'd be that into it anyway. I'll see you back at home?"

"I still smell that old crumpled **meat**," said Waldo. "We will go check the cafeteria. If there is a snack there we will

clean it up. Then we will run in circles in the gym, since the cafeteria and the gymnasium are the same giant room. You meet us there when your paper-clip meeting is over."

Sassy wagged her tail under the trench coat. This was a good plan. At home, Waldo and Sassy were vigilant about cleaning up every dropped **bread crumb** and errant **shred of cheese**. They had often discussed what an excellent and enormous job it must be to clean

PUSH

the floor of the room where so many human children hurriedly and sloppily ate food every day.

"Okay," said Stewart. "If you're sure you want to wait. I'll meet you in the cafeteria in an hour."

"We will not be waiting," said Sassy. "We will be eating."

"If there are for-sure snacks, then next time we will also be enthusiastic about office supplies," said Waldo.

"Do they ever make thumbtacks out of **sausages**?" asked Sassy.

"Probably not," said Stewart.

"They should."

CHAPTER THREE

The dogs left Stewart and made their way down the hallway. The cafeteria was their favorite room in the school besides the classroom (Waldo's choice), the library (still Waldo), the music room (yep, also Waldo), and "any room with a good sun spot to nap in" (that's Sassy's).

The dogs had never been in school after hours before, and walking down the empty hallway made them feel like they knew a secret.

They heard footsteps behind them and turned to see their teacher, Ms. Twohey, wearing a coat and carrying a tote bag. "See you tomorrow, Salty!"

"See you tomorrow!" said Waldo. "Where are you going?"

"Home," said Ms. Twohey.

"You do not live here in Bea Arthur Memorial Elementary School?"

"What? No, of course not. I live in an apartment a few miles from here. Teachers don't live in school."

"That is completely new information!"

"Oh, Salty. You are such a hoot."

Waldo waved at Ms. Twohey as he watched in amazement to see that she did, in fact, leave the school completely.

They walked into the cafeteria/gymnasium/ auditorium and took a deep sniff.

"**Industrial cheese** and **not-fresh meat**!" said Sassy. "I love it so."

"This is definitely the smell of all smells I was smelling," said Waldo.

"What should we do while we're waiting for Stewart to finish with his office supply enthusiasm?" said Sassy.

"I've been waiting for a moment like this," said Waldo. "I want to explore behind the counter."

"We're not allowed to go behind the counter!" said Sassy. "Only lunch-making humans can be behind the counter!"

"They're not here now," said Waldo. "They'll never know. Come on. I'm going behind the counter. You can stay here in the middle of the room if you want."

Waldo started toward the room where the lunches

came from. Every school day, the lunch humans handed the dogs a plate of delicious food over that counter, and every school day, Waldo wondered about what kind of amazing place there must be behind the counter. Were there magical **beef** elves who sprinkled everything, even **salad**, with little bits of **meat**? Was there a **sandwich** fairy who was able to transform the most incongruous ingredients into delicious **sandwiches**? Did a goblin of **cheese** do . . . well, the **cheese** goblin would do something spectacular, obviously. It was always right around the **cheese** goblin part that Waldo got too hungry to continue.

Sassy lay down in the middle of the cafeteria. She was a good dog. She wasn't going to get in trouble. She'd take a nap. Her eyes closed slowly.

"I'm cooooooming, **Cheese** Goblin!" screamed Waldo.

Sassy jumped up. "Wait for me!" she shouted, running and skidding across the floor. "I don't know what goblin **cheese** is, but you better save some for me!"

The dogs nosed open the door that led to the room behind the counter.

"Huh," said Waldo. "There is no **cheese**."

"No, there is not," said Sassy.

As a matter of fact, there wasn't any **food** at all. The whole room was shiny and silver and smelled like bleach. There was a sink and a table. There was a big stove and two enormous silver doors. And they could see how the cafeteria looked from the other side of the counter.

"Look," said Waldo, hopping up on a stool. "I am a cafeteria dog. Hello, imaginary human student. Hello, other imaginary human student. Would you like today's special? It is **beef** with a side of **beef** and a sprinkling of **beef** in a **beef sauce**."

"What do you think is behind these huge doors?" asked Sassy. She pawed at the handles.

"Or perhaps you would like our other special," Waldo continued. "It is **cheese** à la Frisbee, which is an entire Frisbee, upside down, full of **cheese**. It's really great."

"Got it," said Sassy, unlatching a big door and hooking her paw into the opening.

"The best bet today, really, is the double-double-triple," said Waldo to another imaginary student. "That's four servings of the **beef** special and three servings of the **cheese** special, layered on top of one another. It's so much food that we have to wheel it out to you on a special cart!"

Waldo was drooling a little.

He really was very hungry.

Waldo heard a gasp, and then a scraping noise behind him.

"I found it!" Sassy yelled. "The **cheese** goblin exists!"

Sassy had propped open the huge silver doors with a stool, and clouds of cold air were puffing into the room. Waldo peeked in and saw Sassy sitting on the floor of the world's biggest refrigerator, gnawing on the corner of a plastic-wrapped hunk of **cheese** the size of a Yorkshire terrier.

"What is HAPPENING?" said Waldo.

"While you were playing that fun **beef**-and-**cheese** game, I found the Queen's Refrigerator."

"What do you mean, Queen's Refrigerator?"

"This is the refrigerator from a castle, don't you think? No normal, non-royal human person would have a refrigerator this big. Look at all this **food**!" She chewed through the plastic around the **cheese** and got to work eating and licking as much **cheese** as she could.

"Is this what I think it is?" asked Waldo.

"What do you think it is?"

"A dream? Am I dreaming?" Waldo sniffed at a large cardboard box labeled HAMBURGERS. "It smells real enough."

"I think our new plan is that we should live here now," said Sassy. "Have some of this **cheese**. It's the best **cheese** I've ever had."

"You've got **orange melty bits** on your chin. And some plastic. Is plastic food?" asked Waldo.

"Who knows? I'll eat it all and figure that out later. Wait, what's that noise?" Both dogs stood still and listened. Someone was coming.

"Quick, get out of the Queen's Refrigerator!" said Sassy. The dogs ran into the kitchen and shut the big refrigerator doors. Waldo peeked through the window into the cafeteria while he jumped onto Sassy's back and pulled the trench coat over them. There was a boy in a baseball cap wandering around the room. "Ah, it is our good friend Bax. Hello to you, Bax! Do you want to play this **beef**-and-**cheese** lunch-window game with me?"

"I thought I heard a commotion in here," said Bax. "You bet I want to play your game."

ax was the first student the dogs met, besides Stewart. He shared their love of food and throwing balls around, which was all they needed to know he was a top-notch human.

"What are you doing in here, Salty?" asked Bax.

"What are you doing in here, Bax?" asked Waldo.

"Sometimes I come in here to the gym after school to see if there are any balls or Frisbees lying around that need to be put away."

"And then what?"

"And then I put them away."

"Wow, you are the best helper student."

"There, like, look there. There's a kickball in the corner." Bax pointed, and sure enough, a rubber kickball was wedged behind a garbage can.

"I thought something smelled kickbally," said Waldo.

"Sure you did," said Bax, grabbing the ball. "Now watch this."

Bax raised the ball over his head and threw it as hard as he could against the floor. The ball hit the floor with a satisfying *sproing* and bounced high above their heads. Bax ran toward the ball and caught it neatly, and then bounced it on the floor again.

The dogs had never seen anything more mesmerizing.

"This is my new favorite show," said Waldo.

"Sometimes I can do other stuff, like this," said Bax. He bounced the ball again and it arced toward the basketball hoop, knocked against the rim, and flew sideways.

"Wow, you are really good," said Waldo. "No, wait, I can get it in."

Under the trench coat, Sassy sat slowly on the floor so she could paw at the **cheese** stuck to her chin. Waldo watched, riveted, as Bax tried and failed to bounce the kickball into the basketball hoop.

"Okay, never mind that," said Bax. "Watch this!" He dribbled the kickball front and back between his legs, until it hit his sneaker and rolled across the floor.

"Why are you even in school?" said Waldo. "You should go get a job as a professional ball bouncer."

"Pretty sure that's not a thing. Now you tell me what you're doing."

"I'm playing lunch human. I'll show you." Waldo dug his ankle into Sassy's shoulder blade so she'd stand up, and they walked into the kitchen, where Waldo peered back at Bax over the counter.

"Hello, human student," said Waldo. "Would you like lunch? I will offer you a delicious lunch. Would you like **noodles** and **old meat**?"

"Sure, that sounds great," said Bax. "Give me four servings of that."

"Here you go," said Waldo as he pantomimed spooning **noodles** onto an imaginary plate.

"Hoooo, that was fun," said Waldo. "Do you want to pretend to be a different human student, and we'll do it again?"

"Nah," said Bax.

"Are you having to go home now?"

"Nah," said Bax. "I'm supposed to join a club, but I can't decide which club to join."

"A club is a **sandwich**."

"Too bad that's not one of the choices."

"There are other choices?" asked Waldo.

"Card Pyramids, Tea Parties, and Glue Hands."

"What is Glue Hands?" asked Waldo.

"You spread glue on your hands, let it dry, then peel it off," said Bax.

"Then what?"

"It looks like a fake hand."

"We found some **cheese**. It's not shaped like a hand. You should stay in here with us."

"Are you saying what I think you're saying?" asked Bax.

"I do not know. Yes?"

"Awesome."

"It is so awesome," said Waldo.

And that's how Waldo and Sassy ended up starting a club at Bea Arthur Elementary by accident.

CHAPTER FIVE

he first thing we should do," said Waldo, "is explore hidden corners of the cafetorium."

"Why don't they call it an auditoria?" asked Bax.

"It is a mystery," said Waldo. "Do you want to see the Queen's Refrigerator?"

"You bet I do," said Bax. "Lead the way."

Salty showed Bax the giant refrigerator in the kitchen. They showed him the sinks "that are practically big enough to give a bath to five muddy beagles" and the counter that "would fit one thousand sandwiches." They found a freezer behind the big fridge ("the King's Freezer!" said Waldo, wondering how to quickly defrost twenty-five pounds of **ground beef**) and a row of shelves around the corner.

"These cans of **tomato sauce** are bigger than my head," said Bax.

"They are bigger than a Newfoundland's head," said Waldo.

"It's funny how you always measure things in terms of dogs," said Bax.

"I don't."

"Sure you do. I like it. You must really be into dogs."

"Dogs are very in right now."

"Well, yeah," said Bax.

A girl in a lab coat walked briskly into the gym and stopped in her tracks when she saw Bax and Salty.

"What are you doing in here?" she asked.

Bax turned toward the voice. "Oh, hey, Arden. I was looking for a club—"

"A **club sandwich!**" said Waldo, sniffing the air. Sassy jumped to attention under the coat.

"Wait, what are *you* doing in here?" said Bax.

"Not that I need to tell you my business, but I'm getting supplies for my own club."

"**Sandwich**," said Waldo.

"Are there **club sandwiches** up there?" asked Sassy.

"Shhhh, not now," whispered Waldo. Sassy slumped underneath him.

"What?" said Arden. She opened the equipment closet and pulled out a basket of tennis balls.

"**You have a tennis balls club!**" said Waldo.

"No, we need them for training," said Arden. Then she said some more things, something about proving herself, something about needing to show that she's responsible, and something else about practicing a lot. There might have been a part about **cookies**. It was hard to tell. Waldo stopped listening once he saw all the tennis balls.

"We will be in your tennis balls club!" said Waldo.

"Wait, no, you're here with me," said Bax.

"You can be in tennis balls with Arfen!"

"It's Arden," said Arden, "and it's not a tennis ball club."

"Fine. We will stay here and think about sandwiches," said Waldo.

"Are there club sandwiches up there?" said Sassy.

"Yeah, we will," said Bax. They both watched as Arden left with her tennis ball basket. "Now what?"

"Let's run really fast in circles," said Waldo.

"Yeah!" said Bax. "I love doing that!"

"I better get my **sandwich** after this run," Sassy whispered up to Waldo.

Bax and Salty ran in circles and figure eights around the wide perimeter of the room, until Bax, panting, collapsed against the wall.

"**You are good at that**," said Waldo.

"So are you," said Bax. "That's fun. We still have ten minutes. What should we do now?"

"**You tell me. I do not always have to be the activity picker.**"

"Sure you do. Or, I mean, I guess I could come up with something. If you told me to."

"What we should do is nap for just a little bit," said Waldo.

"That's the best plan yet." Bax leaned his head back against the yellow cinder block wall.

"Hey, what are you doing in here? Why are you so sweaty?" The gym teacher, who everyone called Coach, came in dragging an enormous mesh bag of soccer balls.

"We were doing a running type of exercise," said Waldo.

"Good work, team! What are you doing now?" asked Coach.

"Sleeping," said Bax.

"Digesting cheese," said Waldo, making prolonged eye contact with the bag of balls.

"Not eating a **sandwich**," said Sassy to herself.

"Can I get you two to put these balls in the closet? I'd do it myself, but I like delegating."

"**I like delegating too**," said Waldo.

"You do?" said Coach.

"**Sure**," said Waldo. Waldo whispered to Sassy. "What is delegating? Is it a kind of **casserole**?"

"You have **casserole** up there too?" said Sassy.

"Just put these balls away. You're a good kid. I have to go do push-ups." Coach blew his whistle, did a few jumping jacks, and left.

"I like having a job," said Waldo. "We will put these balls away. That is our job."

Bax continued napping while Waldo and Sassy dragged the balls toward the closet. They got halfway before they became overwhelmed by soccer-ball aroma. Bax woke up just before they were about to give up and chew on all the balls, and he helped drag them the rest of the way.

"Well, this was a lot of fun," said Bax. "I'm glad I found you."

"Yes, me too," said Waldo. "Eating the queen's cheese is more fun with three."

"With two, you mean."

"Either way."

"Hey, you guys," said Stewart from the doorway. "Are you ready to go home?"

"Oh, is Stewart the third cheese eater?" said Bax.

"Okay," said Waldo.

"What?" said Stewart.

"Never mind," said Bax. "See you tomorrow!"

CHAPTER SIX

We are sorry we were not able to stay with you," said Waldo on the walk home, "but it was too many pencils and not enough **meatballs**. Did you have fun?"

"It was all right," said Stewart. "We made a sticky-note mosaic and talked about what the best highlighter color is."

"What *is* the best highlighter color?" asked Sassy.

"Yellow," said Stewart. "Though Melanie said it was green."

"Did Mr. Nehi ever give you snacks?" asked Waldo.

"At the end he gave us tiny cups of **cherry tomatoes**."

"Fun!" said Waldo.

"I guess."

"Tiny cups of snacks are fun!" said Waldo.

"As long as there are four hundred tiny cups," said Sassy.

"Tomorrow we're going to talk about index cards," said Stewart.

"Gosh," said Waldo. "Your club sounds amazing."

"Really?"

"You're the best human, so any club you're in is going to be so great."

"Well, yeah. Thanks. Does that mean you're coming to the next meeting?" asked Stewart.

"Maybe we will," said Sassy. "I do not think index cards are fun, but we always have fun with you."

"Especially if there are snacks," added Waldo.

"You know what we should do?" said Sassy. "We should forget about clubs and just come home for snacks like we have always done!"

"Sassy, that's a great idea!" said Waldo. "Then we can nap and snack and keep the squirrels out like always. You solved everything."

"I don't think that solves anything," said Stewart. "I still have to go to Junior Office Supply Enthusiasts."

"Do you?" asked Waldo. "You smell like you don't really want to go."

Stewart's parents were both waiting at the door when Stewart and the dogs got home.

"Look at them, waiting for us," said Waldo. "They are like dogs."

The parents were bouncing. They were excited.

"How was it?" said Stewart's mom, hugging him.

"Wow, what is happening?" said Waldo, sniffing.

"Some **meat** exploded all over the kitchen table," said Sassy.

"What's all this?" asked Stewart. The table had a white tablecloth over it and candles were lit. The good plates were out, and each plate had a cloth napkin folded into the shape of a stapler on it.

"Today was your first day of Junior Office Supply Enthusiasts!" said Stewart's dad. "That calls for a celebration!"

"We made a **roast ham** and **baby broccoli**, and **chocolate cake** for dessert!"

"Wow," said Stewart. "That's great. I mean, okay. It's only office supplies."

"That's hilarious!" said Stewart's dad. "'Only office supplies!' That's like saying 'It's only breathing' or 'It's just my heart beating.'"

"Our little jokester!" said Stewart's mom. "Now, sit down! Eat! Tell us everything!"

"Well. We talked about highlighters."

"YOU ARE SO LUCKY," said Stewart's dad. "I love highlighters so much."

"Highlighters are such a vital part of human society," said Stewart's mom.

"They tell you that you already read something, *and* they tell you what the important parts of that thing are," said Stewart's dad.

"Sometimes there's an important document that needs to be signed," said Stewart's mom. "And you highlight the words *Sign Here* so that everyone knows where to sign it."

"Although sometimes there are sticky notes that are shaped like arrows, and you can stick one of those on the document, pointing to the signing line," said Stewart's dad.

"We talked about sticky notes too," said Stewart.

"YOU ARE SO LUCKY!" said both of his parents.

His mom sighed happily. "And sometimes, you can highlight *Sign Here* AND put the sticky-note arrow on the paper."

His dad put his hands on his heart. "You are so right, honey. That's the best."

"The parents like office supplies like we like **meatballs**," Sassy said to Waldo.

"My favorite **meat** is the kind they are having right now."

"**Roast ham**?"

"Yes."

"When did you have **roast ham**?"

"Never. But I can smell that it is my favorite," said Waldo.

"Waldo?"

"Yes."

"I don't think Stewart likes his club like we like **roast ham**."

"I know," said Waldo. "He does not smell like he's in love with highlighter pens."

"We should go with him again tomorrow, to make it more fun," said Sassy.

"He always has fun when we're around!"

"Should we bring tiny cups of snacks tomorrow?" asked Sassy.

"Oh! Yes! We definitely should!" said Waldo.
"What should we put in the tiny cups?"
"**Roast ham**."

CHAPTER SEVEN

H ow are you all coming along with your stories?" Ms. Twohey asked the class. They had been working on elements of fiction, and everyone was writing and revising a story.

"My story is so great," said Bax.

"Would you like to read us what you have so far?"

Bax walked to the front of the class and read from his story. It was called "Lair of the Den of the Fortress of **Hot Dogs**" and was mostly a detailed description of how to build a house out of **hot dogs**, and how convenient it would be if you ran out of **food**, since your

house was made of **hot dogs**. Also there was a battle scene where the hero, who was also named Bax, threw **hot dogs** at his enemy.

"That was the most exciting and delicious story I have ever heard," Waldo said to Bax when Bax finished reading.

"You bet it was," said Bax.

Arden went next. Her story was about a girl named Lacybelle who was extremely accomplished and won a lot of awards, and also lived on a farm with a lot of farm animals, except all the farm animals were dogs. The dogs provided Lacybelle with affection, teamwork, and fur to be knit into sweaters. They did plumbing repairs and helped build a fence. One of them sang Lacybelle a lullaby every night.

"And Lacybelle and her dogs lived happily ever after," said Arden.

"Wow, that was very exciting!" said Waldo. "Also I am wondering if you have ever met a dog."

"Of course I've met a dog," said Arden. "Sheesh. It's supposed to be a fantasy."

"Salty, would you like to read your story?" asked Ms. Twohey.

"You bet I would!"

Sassy yawned and stood up. She stretched. Waldo started to fall off her and lunged for a pencil and pretended that was what he meant to do all along. Sassy walked to the front of the room. Waldo cleared his throat and began to read.

"Once upon a **meatball**, there was a great detective. He was a very good detective. He knew he was a good detective because everyone always said, 'Good job! Good detective!' He was the best at finding criminal squirrels on the streets of Squirreltown. His name was Rover Scout, and this is his story. Rover Scout was sitting in his office one day talking on a cell phone and heating **soup** in a microwave and doing other human things. A very nice lady came in and said, 'Oh, Rover Scout, thank goodness! You have to help me find my **hamburgers**! I had a whole truck full of **hamburgers** and Someone stole it!'"

"Okay, Salty, that's a great start, thank you," said Ms. Twohey.

"But I was just getting to the good part," said Waldo.

"I know, but we have to give other people a turn too."

"Oh. Okay." The dogs sat down.

"Yo, that story was great," Bax whispered to Waldo. "Rover Scout! That's a great name."

"I will read you the part about **hamburgers** later, if you want," said Waldo.

"If we have time," said Bax. "We have a lot to do."

"**We do?**"

"Probably. Running in circles and stuff."

"**I love running in circles!**"

"Bax and Salty, are you quite done?" asked Ms. Twohey pointedly. "Or is there something you want to share with the class?"

"Sorry, Ms. T," said Bax. "Just discussing club stuff."

"**A club is a sandwich**," said Waldo.

"A **sandwich** I never get to taste," said Sassy.

"Did you bring a whole **sandwich** for snack time?" said Ms. Twohey.

"**I wish I brought a sandwich**," said Waldo. "**I brought this block of cheese the size of a corgi snout.**"

"*We* brought the **cheese**," said Sassy from underneath the coat.

Bax turned around to the students sitting behind him. "You should come to our club," said Bax. "It's the coolest."

"Do you know what you're going to do for your float?" asked a girl named Piper.

"**Root beer float**," said Waldo.

"It's a great club," said Bax. "There are games and educational field trips and exercise."

"That sounds like what we did yesterday!" said Waldo.

"Do we get badges to put on a sash?" asked Piper.

"Badgers on a sash is so fun," said Waldo. "I want sash badgers."

"No, badges," said Piper. "You know, like the scouts have. Your merit badge and your hiking badge and cookie badge."

"Hey, we can be the Rover Scouts!" said Bax.

"Rover Scout is my detective name!" said Waldo.

"Right, I know," said Bax.

"When do I get a **cookie** badger?" asked Waldo.

"Save some **cookie** badger for me!" said Sassy.

CHAPTER EIGHT

A fter school, the dogs went with Stewart to Junior Office Supply Enthusiasts.

"Today will be better," said Waldo. "We brought snacks!"

He patted his backpack. They went into the classroom and found a spot where Mr. Nehi had not yet laid out organized piles of index cards. Waldo opened the bag. It was full of tiny snack cups.

Empty tiny snack cups.

"**Pardon me for a moment**," said Waldo. He stuck his head down into the trench coat. "Where are all the cheese bits and scavenged **roast ham** shreds?"

"In my stomach," whispered Sassy.

"Everything okay, Salty?" asked Mr. Nehi.

"No," said Waldo. "There are no snacks."

"If we have time after index cards, we'll have **crackers**," said Mr. Nehi. "Though I can't make any promises. We all know how much there is to say about index cards!"

"Stewart, we are sorry," said Waldo. "But we need snacks. We will meet you in the cafegymnoria in one hour."

"Yeah, I know," said Stewart. "It's all right."

The dogs were surprised to find Bax, Piper, and four other students waiting in the cafeteria.

"There you are!" said Bax. "Rover Scouts, reporting for duty!"

"That's my detective name," said Waldo.

"Right, I know," said Bax. "What should we do first?"

"First we play lunch line," said Waldo, standing behind the window in the kitchen. Piper came up to the window.

"Student. Hello," said Waldo. "Would you like nine hamburgers?"

"I would like eight hamburgers," said Piper.

"Why not nine?" asked Waldo.

"Nine is too many."

"Nine is not too many," said Waldo. "Nine might not even be enough."

"I think eighteen is a good number of hamburgers," said Bax. "I'm hungry."

"Oh! Just a moment!" said Waldo. "Snack time!"

Sassy walked Waldo over to the shelves in the kitchen. "Should we eat that can of **vanilla pudding**?"

Waldo thought for a moment. "I think," he said, "that we will not be able to work the can opener."

"Maybe we should climb on that counter, grab the **pudding** can, and throw it on the ground. Then it will smash into bits and we can all lick up the **pudding**."

Waldo looked out into the cafeteria. "Piper does not quite seem like the type of student who would lick **vanilla pudding** off the floor."

"Sure she does," said Sassy. "But let's look in the Queen's Refrigerator."

The dogs assembled a snack tray of **red peppers** and **croutons** and brought it back over to the group. Everyone grabbed a handful.

"Now, **after snack time, we will nap**," said Waldo.

"Rover Scouts is fun!" said Piper.

"Hey, what are you kids doing in here?" It was Dottie, the school secretary.

"We are having our club meeting," said Bax.

"Oh, did you bring a **sandwich**?" asked Waldo.

"Pass me the **bread** and also the filling if there's a **sandwich**, Waldo," said Sassy.

"What's your club?" asked Dottie.

"Rover Scouts," said Bax.

"Rover Scout is my detective name," said Waldo.

"You're not on the official list."

"You should put us on the official list," said Bax. "We are an official club. We are maybe newer than others. But we are very official. We have members and a name."

"You'll have to fill out these forms. And here's a packet of information about Founders Day. And you can't be in here. The Founders Day planning committee is about to meet."

"That's cool," said Bax. "We'll go outside."

The Rover Scouts went to the playground behind the school. Sassy sat down. She was tired, and sometimes it was hard for her to stay awake, since it was so dark and warm under the trench coat. And there were no **club sandwiches** in there like on the outside where Waldo was. And sometimes it was hard to nap when Waldo wanted her to be his legs.

"Now we **run in circles**," said Waldo. "To **digest**."

"What about napping?" said Bax.

"**We will maybe nap in between activities. Or maybe a big one at the end. I don't know. You tell me.**"

"No, you have to tell us," said Bax. "You're the leader."

"The leader of what?"

"I'm going to win!" yelled Piper, and she started running in circles around the baseball diamond. Bax, Salty, and the other kids chased after her.

They ran in circles for a few minutes and then spread out on the grass for napping.

"Now what?" said Bax, after they had napped for a bit.

"Let's go smell things," said Waldo.

"What?" said Piper.

"I'll show you," said Waldo. They walked over to a tree. Waldo breathed in forcefully through his nose. "Now you do it."

All the students breathed in deeply. A girl named Susan had a coughing fit. They waited for her to stop coughing, and then they breathed some more.

"I can smell a tree," said Piper.

"I can smell the grass," said Susan.

"I smell squirrels," said Bax. A squirrel chattered at them and jumped from one branch to another.

"That is good," said Waldo. "I smell tennis balls."

The students looked around. There were no tennis balls. Just then Arden and her club came walking across the field.

"I bet I was smelling the tennis balls that Arden has," said Waldo.

"Why are you all staring at me?" said Arden.

Bax explained that their club was doing an exercise about smelling. Waldo wanted to know why Bax was talking about **sandwiches** again. Sassy wanted to know why everyone outside the coat was always getting **sandwiches** and she never got any.

Arden looked at the group of kids smelling things in front of her. "Our club is *so* going to win the parade."

"Do *you* have a **sandwich**?" asked Waldo.

"I know I don't," said Sassy.

"There you are!" said Stewart.

"Oh, Stewart, hooray!" said Waldo. Sassy sat down so no one would see her tail wagging. She had trouble controlling her tail around Stewart.

"Are you ready to go?"

"Yes," said Waldo. He turned to the other students. "Maybe I will see you tomorrow! We can do more fun things!"

"See you tomorrow, Rover Salty!"

"Rover Salty! That sounds like my detective name!"

"What was all that rover stuff?" asked Stewart as they walked home.

"I guess everyone really liked my detective story," said Waldo.

CHAPTER NINE

After they got home from school, Stewart sat on his bed reading. Waldo napped by Stewart's feet. Sassy kept trying to sleep on a pile of laundry on the floor, but then she'd get very comfortable and slide off, which would wake her up. It was exhausting. Finally she stood up and looked at Stewart.

"Thank you for letting us come to your school," she said.

"Oh, you're welcome," said Stewart. "Even though I didn't really let you. You just showed up one day."

"You could have told us 'bad dogs' and made us go home."

"You're not bad dogs. I wouldn't do that."

"You said I was a bad dog when I removed all the garbage from the can in the kitchen because there was a piece of **bacon**," said Waldo.

"Yeah," said Stewart.

"You said I was a bad dog when I was sorting laundry and accidentally ate most of the shirt that you got at Camp Weeksofun."

"Well," said Stewart.

"And you said we were bad dogs when we were so helpful that time, when we helped clean the kitchen counter of all that **meat** someone had left there," said Waldo.

"You ate the entire **Thanksgiving turkey**!" said Stewart.

"You're welcome," said Waldo.

"Okay, so maybe you do naughty things sometimes, but you're both really good dogs."

"And you're the best boy," said Sassy. "How is your pencil club going?"

"Yes," said Waldo. "Tell us."

"Oh, it's great," said Stewart.

"We want it to be great," said Waldo. "But you smell bored and nervous."

"No, really, it's fine," said Stewart, somewhat convincingly. "Paper clips are cool. They come in all different sizes, and sometimes even in different colors."

"Wow, that is neato!" said Waldo. "And sometimes they are made of **cheese**!"

"No, actually."

"You know who would really like this club?" said Waldo. "Your parents. This is stuff they get really excited about."

"Yeah. They've always loved office supplies."

"Can they go? They should go to the club. They would be so happy."

"It's for Junior Office Supply Enthusiasts," said Stewart. "They are lifetime members of Office Supply Enthusiasts, which is the one for grown-ups."

"Once, your mom talked about pencils for forty-five minutes," said Waldo.

"That sounds about right," said Stewart.

"Remember that time they spent a Sunday afternoon writing a song about composition notebooks?" said Sassy.

"Yeah," said Stewart. "You know, it is kind of fun. Today I made a paper-clip chain that was three feet long. Maybe you two should come try the club again. I know there aren't snacks, but you could play with office supplies."

"Maybe we will," said Waldo. "Though we have fun playing with other human students when the school is empty."

"It is great," said Sassy. "There is a lot of running and smelling things."

Waldo started pacing and grumbling.

"This is a tough decision," said Waldo. "On the one paw, we always want to be with you, Stewart. On the other paw, playing in the cafeteria is fun. On the third paw, snacks are important. On the fourth paw, I have trouble doing pencil and paper-clip work."

Sassy sat up and barked. "I know! Stewart! You should come play in the cafeteria with us!"

"Oh," said Stewart. "Yeah. I can't. I have to stay in Junior Office Supply Enthusiasts."

"But if it is not what you want, then you should switch!" said Waldo.

"Remember when one time you got us that different **kibble**?" said Sassy. "How we had **chicken kibbles** for years and years and then one day for no reason at all you got us **tuna kibbles**?" The memory of the **tuna** incident always put Sassy on edge.

"And we did not like it," said Waldo. "Remember, we said, 'We are not cats!'" Waldo also did not like to think about it.

"Yeah, I remember that. You two were a real pain about those **tuna kibbles**. They were out of the **chicken**. That's why I had to get you a different kind."

"But the school is not out of clubs," said Waldo. "You don't have to do binder-clip club because it's the only one. There are lots of clubs."

"Yeah," said Stewart. "I know."

"Maybe you should get your parents **tuna**," said Sassy. "Then they would understand about clubs."

"They would *really* get it. That **tuna** was not for dogs!" said Waldo, shaking his head repeatedly.

"I don't know if it works that way," said Stewart. "But I'll think about it. You both seem pretty worked up," said Stewart. "Let's go to the park before dinner."

"Yes, please," said Waldo.

"I need to zoom-in-circles the **tuna** away," said Sassy.

CHAPTER TEN

Stewart opened the gate to the dog park and the other dogs ran to them.

"How's the school racket going?" said Tugboat, a big gray dog with fluffy ears.

"It's great," said Waldo.

"Tell me again how it works!" said Pistachio. "Tell me tell me tell me!"

"You need to dial down your **coffee** intake," said Sassy.

Pistachio chased her tail for a minute. "Oh, I have to introduce you to my imaginary brother!"

Sassy turned to the air next to Pistachio. "Pleased to meet you."

"No, he's not invisible, silly silly silly, he's just not my real brother. He's my brother for a little while."

Pistachio led the dogs over to the humans, who were standing in a clump. They were looking at their phones. Some were talking. Some were drinking coffee. Stewart had climbed a tree. There was a scrawny white terrier sitting nervously near one of the humans' feet. He stood up when he saw Pistachio.

"Everyone, this is Jeffy," said Pistachio. "He's staying at my house until he can move into his regular house."

"Where's your regular house?" asked Waldo.

Jeffy looked at the ground. "I don't know yet."

"What is Jeffy short for?" asked Buttercup.

"Why does it have to be short for something?" asked Tugboat. "Maybe it's long for Jeff."

"It's short for Jefferton," said Pistachio, standing protectively in front of Jeffy. "Everyone in his litter was named after a president."

"Jefferton's not a—" said Buttercup.

"Yes it is! Tobias Jefferton! He was the . . . third president of the town of the things and stuff and the country. But enough about that, let's talk about school some more." Pistachio turned to Jeffy to explain. "Waldo and Sassy pretend to be a human student at school all day long every day and they're like spies and secret agents and they know all the secrets."

"It is very fun," said Waldo. "We read stories and learn new vocabulary. There is science and gym."

"Forget about all that," said Buttercup. "You know what we really want to hear about."

"Tell us!" barked Pistachio. "Tell us tell us tell us about LUNCH."

"Everything you heard is true," said Sassy. "The lunch is huge and **meaty** and sometimes covered in **cheese**."

"Is it really every single day?" asked Tugboat. "Not just sometimes?"

"Every day!" said Waldo.

The other dogs sat in contemplative awe.

"Is it true that sometimes you get a **sandwich**?" asked Buttercup. "Tell us about **sandwiches**."

"There's **turkey** and **cheese**," said Sassy. "And **ham** and **cheese**. **Egg salad**, that's a good one. And probably others. Waldo talks about **sandwiches** when he's standing on top of me, and I don't know if there are some he eats without sharing."

"I share them all!" said Waldo. "**Grilled cheese** is a nice one too. And there's a **chicken sandwich** where the **chicken** is a piece of **fried chicken**."

"**Fried chicken**!" said Pistachio. "**Fried chicken fried chicken**! **Fried chicken** between **bread** pieces?"

"Yes!" said Waldo.

"Wow," said all the dogs in wonder.

"But the best thing of all," said Sassy, "is the **cheeseburger**."

"Yes," said Waldo as all the dogs listened raptly.

"The **cheeseburger**! It's a piece of **meat**—"
"Ooooh," said the dogs.

"And a piece of **melted cheese**."
"Woooowww," said the dogs.

"And a big, fluffy **bread bun**."

"It's too much," said Buttercup. "You get to eat so many good things on one plate."

"And the humans get that every day!" said Tugboat. "It's not fair! I want lunch!"

"To get lunch, you have to do math," said Pistachio.

"I don't want math," said Tugboat. "I just want lunch."

"You are heroes," said Buttercup, "for learning about lunch. I don't think I could go to school all day. If only there was a way for me to get lunch without giving up my all-day nap."

"All you have to do is find a trench coat," said Waldo.

At the mention of the trench coat, Sassy remembered how tiring it was to hold Waldo up all day, and she started to run in circles again. Waldo grabbed a stick and chased her, and then Pistachio jumped onto a bench and yelled at everyone. Jeffy didn't join in the running, but he got closer to their looping circles and wagged once or twice when everyone came close.

Stewart called his dogs and said it was time to go. They said goodbye to their dog park pals.

"I hope you find your regular house soon!" Sassy told Jeffy.

"Maybe my new home will be the school and I'll get lunch too," said Jeffy.

CHAPTER ELEVEN

Hey, what are you doing?" Stewart asked the dogs when he came into his room after dinner. The dogs were lying on the floor, surrounded by papers and colored pencils.

"Dottie the secretary gave us homework because she is our friend," said Waldo.

"And even though we have done so much school in our lives," said Sassy, "this homework is hard. It is a lot of writing down answers on tiny lines. Dottie called it 'a packet of forms and paperwork.'"

"We thought a packet was going to be like a **sandwich**," said Waldo. "But it's not."

"It really sounds like a **sandwich**!" said Sassy.

"There's a whole month of the Junior Office Supply Enthusiasts devoted to forms and paperwork," said Stewart, flopping on the bed.

"Do you want to practice now with these forms?" asked Waldo. "You know what they say: Practice makes **pizza**."

"Nah," said Stewart. "What is all this anyway?" he asked, picking up some of the papers. "This is weird. These are forms to establish a club."

"That *is* weird," said Sassy.

"It is because Dottie is our friend," said Waldo, "and she knows how much we like homework."

"Well, that's cool," said Stewart. He picked up some of the forms and read them while the dogs worked on filling them out. It was more fun than doing his own homework.

"This form has what I think is an essay on the importance of napping?" said Stewart.

"That's right," said Waldo.

"This form asks what your club's guiding principle is, and it looks like you wrote '**pepperoni hot dog** fun.'"

"Yes," said Sassy.

"And on this part that asks if you need any special equipment, you drew a fork and stuck on a recipe for **meatloaf**."

"Correct," said Waldo.

"We are doing a good job of filling out the forms," said Sassy.

"Are you sure you don't want to fill out some of these forms?" said Waldo. "It would be good practice for your club. Unless you decided you want to play with us and the other human students in the gymnatoria after school. It would be top-notch **meat** town if you were there too."

"I have to go to Junior Office Supply Enthusiasts tomorrow. We're doing glue sticks. My mom said that one's a blast."

"I used a glue stick to attach the **meatloaf** recipe," said Sassy. "We can show you how!"

"It's higher-level glue stick information," said Stewart. "Special topics in glue stick technology."

Sassy was getting very sleepy. Filling out all those forms was hard work. She sprawled out on the bed and yawned.

"You don't smell like you want to play with glue sticks," she said.

"We're almost done with all this homework," said Waldo. "All we have to do is fill out this form about a float."

"Whatever that is," said Sassy.

CHAPTER TWELVE

The next day in class, Arden turned around to tell Bax all about her float.

"It's going to be amazing," she said. "If our float routine works the way I hope it does, I'll get what I've wanted my entire life."

"What's that, world domination?" asked Bax.

"Ha, well, maybe," said Arden. "But no. You'll see. Let's just say that I started this club for a reason."

"Is that what you're doing with all those tennis balls?"

"You'll see. I'm working out the final detail, and then it will all be perfect."

"What's the final detail?" asked Bax.

"I don't know if I should tell you."

"Aw, come on. What am I going to do, steal your idea? How could I even do that, if it's all so cool and perfect?"

"Yeah, you're right, you could never pull it off." Arden leaned in close. "The final detail is dogs."

Waldo's head snapped around. "Dogs?"

"It's going to be great," said Arden.

"It's true, we're not going to have dogs on our float at all," said Bax.

Waldo looked at Bax and wondered where he had gotten a float. And what a float was.

"What is your float going to be?" asked Arden.

"I think I know," said Waldo. "First you get a big glass. Then you scoop in some ice cream, and lick the spoon–"

"Not that kind of float," said Arden.

"Oh, are you talking about the other kind of float?" said Waldo. "Hmm." Waldo didn't know there was another kind of float.

"Our float is so great too, isn't it, Stewart?" said a girl. "When I found out they were starting a Junior Office Supply Enthusiasts club here I almost dropped my binder-clip organizer, I was so excited. Can you believe it? We get to play with pencils!"

"Yeah," said Stewart.

"What is your float?" asked Arden.

"It has office supplies!" said the girl.

"We're totally going to win," said Arden.

"Technically, I don't even have a club yet," said Ralph.

"You should come to ours," said Bax. "It's mostly food."

"Food is important," said Waldo. "Back in Liver, Ohio, if you didn't eat food, you'd die."

"Yeah, that's how it is here too," said Bax.

"We're not so different, you and me," said Waldo.

"We both like naps and snacks," said Bax.

"I wish there was a place called Nap 'n' Snack," said Waldo. "That would be everything you need."

"Look no further," said Bax. "Because that's pretty much what Rover Scouts is."

"That's my detective name!" said Waldo.

Bax stood up, went over to Ralph, and started whispering. Next he went to Charlie and then worked his way around the room, whispering and gesturing to students.

"Bax, what are you doing?" asked Ms. Twohey. "You're supposed to be working on your spelling words."

"Recruiting," said Bax. "I mean, socializing. Spelling! That's what I'm doing. Spelling."

"Well, finish up. The day's almost over."

The class was supposed to be studying how to spell *exaggerate, envelope, pangolin,* and *whippoorwill,* but everyone kept whispering about clubs and floats. Ms. Twohey ignored the whispers. She was sharpening pencils and checking off important boxes in her big spiral-bound teacher's notebook. At one point she looked skyward wistfully.

"I sure did love my time as a Junior Office Supply Enthusiast," she said to no one in particular. "Those were some of the best days of my life."

"You are one of the pencil lickers!" said Waldo. "Did you get your highlighter badger? Some clubs have badgers."

"Uh, no," said Ms. Twohey. "Are you in Junior Office Supply Enthusiasts, Salty?"

"No, I'm not in a club," said Waldo.

"Oh, that's a shame. Clubs are terrific."

"My best friend, Stewart, does the pencil-lickers club. He has all the badgers. I have a cafeteria playdate with six other human students for the hour after school while I wait for Stewart to be done. He doesn't make sausage thumbtacks."

"Sometimes I have no idea what you're talking about, Salty," said Ms. Twohey.

"I'm from Liver, Ohio."

"Well, you really should consider joining a club," said Ms. Twohey. "They foster teamwork and cooperation."

"I couldn't find one that fostered snack-work and food preparation."

"Some of my best memories are from when I helped my club build our float for the Founders Day parade."

"**Root beer float**," said Waldo.

"Which reminds me." Ms. Twohey called for the whole class's attention. "Remember all your club floats must be finished by next Friday. If you don't have them completed before the deadline, you can't enter them into the parade. Founders Day is an important tradition for our town and it's an honor to be able to take part in it."

The bell rang.

"Come on, Salty," said Bax. "Time for Rover Scouts!"

"What's Rover Scouts?" asked Ms. Twohey.

"It's totally a club," said Bax.

"You are so funny!" said Waldo. "It's my detective name. Bax really loves my detective story."

"Whatever," said Bax. "Come on, let's go tackle today's agenda!"

"It sounds like you're in a club," said Ms. Twohey.

"That's ridiculous!" said Waldo. "I would know if I was in a club."

CHAPTER THIRTEEN

Hey, I brought **popcorn** today," said Bax. "So we don't have to go into the kitchen for food."

"That is great news," said Waldo. "You will get your snack-bringer badger for sure."

"When are we getting these badgers?" asked Charlie. "I mean, badges."

"You make it yourself. And then you also get the badger badger," said Waldo.

"Let's tackle this **popcorn**." Bax opened the bag and started throwing the **popcorn** up in the air to catch with his open mouth.

"Wow, you are as good at throwing **popcorn** into your mouth as you are at bouncing balls into the basketball hoop," said Waldo. "I like how many of them fall onto the ground."

Sassy moved closer to Bax and squatted a bit so she could eat all the fallen **popcorn**.

"Thanks," said Bax. "I practice."

"Everyone, we are playing a new fun game where we throw snacks at our faces!" said Waldo.

The students each grabbed a handful of **popcorn** and tossed it in the air, successfully getting it in their own mouths approximately 12 percent of the time.

"You are all doing great!" said Waldo, while Sassy was practically running from fallen snack to fallen snack. "Now you all go outside!"

"Why aren't you coming outside too?" asked Susan.

"I will be *right there*," said Waldo.

The other students left the cafeteria and Waldo frantically hopped off Sassy's back so he could eat as much fallen **popcorn** as possible. There wasn't much left. She'd eaten most of it.

"You ate all the **popcorn**!" said Waldo.

"You get all the **club sandwiches**," said Sassy.

"I told you, there aren't as many **sandwiches** as you think."

"Well, you still get to talk about the **sandwiches**."

Sassy sat down. It was hard being the bottom half of Salty. She had to hold Waldo up all day, and he got all the fun of making eye contact with humans. He

got first pick of the better half of lunch before he casually dropped the rest on the floor for Sassy to eat. And more than once he claimed to have forgotten to drop half of lunch on the floor, and she had to survive on leftovers from Stewart's lunch, which wasn't fair at all. They were always talking about food outside the coat, and Sassy missed out on all that. Waldo got to carry the lunch tray, he got to talk to Ms. Twohey and Dottie and Coach and all their new human friends. None of those humans, except Stewart, even knew Sassy existed.

"Get up. I hear someone coming. We can talk about this later," said Waldo. They jumped back into the coat.

"Hey, Salty, what's taking so long?" said Charlie, from the door.

Salty walked outside.

"We saw Arden's group doing something with tennis balls in the field again, so we're just talking about how bouncy tennis balls are," said Bax.

"I like throwing tennis balls at trees," said Ralph.

"That is a great activity, because you get to throw a ball and also potentially dislodge a squirrel," said Waldo.

"I wish we had some of those tennis balls. She took them all out of the closet again," said Bax.

"You should have tried begging for some. That is a good way to get tennis balls," said Waldo.

"What would we need to beg for?" asked Piper.

"It works for anything," said Waldo. "Food, mostly. But really almost anything can be made easier with a well-timed beg."

"Begging, like when you say please a lot? I'm good at that," said Bax.

"That is one way to do it. But it is more effectory if you add sad eyes," said Waldo.

"What do you mean, sad eyes?" asked Susan.

"I will show you," said Waldo. Waldo thought about all the things he really wanted. He wanted so many things. **Sandwiches**. Chewy bones. Soft beds. Shoes with rubber soles. **Kitchen garbage**. While he was thinking about all the things he wanted so much, he also thought about looking very sad so that humans

would give him everything. He raised his eyebrows a little. He looked up and made his eyes big. He tried to cry, which didn't work, because dogs can't cry.

"Awwwwww!" said all the Rover Scouts.

"Now you try," said Waldo.

The Rover Scouts stood in a line and tried very hard to look sad, and like they needed something very much, with varying degrees of success. Bax was the best.

"Awwwww," said Waldo. "You all are very ador-able and I would give you whatever you wanted if I had anything to give. Which I do not."

"Maybe we can beg someone to help with our float?" said Charlie.

"Yeah, we really have to get on that," said Piper. "We keep talking about food. Which is great. But at some point we need to figure out our float."

"My brother is in Ping-Pong Club and he says they're almost done," said Ralph. "Technically, we haven't even figured out what our float is going to be."

"You all are using a lot of words," said Waldo. "I am from Liver, Ohio."

"Exactly. We don't need to talk about it, we just need to do it. We'll have the best float of all!" said Bax.

CHAPTER FOURTEEN

The next morning, on their way to school, Stewart smelled like a combination of lost homework and the feeling of watching the **ice cream** truck drive away.

"Stewart, are you not happy this morning? The sun is shining like a bright, hot **meatball**," said Sassy.

"Did you forget to eat **bacon** for breakfast?" asked Waldo. "I forgot to do that."

"We didn't have **bacon**," said Stewart.

"I know, you forgot to give it to us," said Waldo. "We forgot to have **bacon**. We forgot to have **sandwiches**. We forgot to have **root beer floats**."

Stewart laughed. "Funny enough, it does have to do with a float, just not that kind. They're giving out assignments for the Junior Office Supply Enthusiasts float today."

"You will be great in any part because you are great at every part," said Sassy.

"I have a question," said Waldo. "This float for Founders Day, it's not a big deal, is it?"

"Uh, it's a huge deal, actually," said Stewart.

They made their way to their classroom.

"Good morning, Stewart. Good morning, Salty," said Ms. Twohey.

"**Good morning, MS. Twohey,**" Waldo and Stewart said together.

The morning announcements started over the loudspeaker. Ms. Barkenfoff, who smelled like tartan skirts and cough drops, listed a bunch of upcoming events before getting to the Founders Day parade.

"And remember, the float deadline is next week. Our very own Mayor Pennywhistle will be presiding over the parade as Grand Marshall."

"The Grunge **Marshmallow**?" said Waldo. "That is a new treat."

Waldo heard Arden groan a couple of chairs over.

"...and we want to make sure our school has a great showing! Barkenfoff out." The principal's voice clicked off from the speaker.

Ms. Twohey stood in front of the class. "I hope everyone is taking part in this wonderful opportunity. The Founders Day parade and float contest is the pinnacle of the whole year!"

Waldo raised his hand. "Everyone always talks about Founders Day all day! Humans are

So focused. Maybe there will be food at Founders Day."

"Yes, there is a whole street lined with concession stands on Founders Day."

"You would think someone would have mentioned that before," said Waldo.

"Well, the float contest and the parade are really what people focus on."

"Why?"

"Because they celebrate the spirit of creativity and ingenuity on which this town was founded," said Ms. Twohey.

"But didn't the founders also have to eat?"

"I suppose."

"I am very excited about this parade now that I know it will be adjacent to food."

"You seem hungry. Are you ready for snack time already, Salty?"

"You are such a good teacher because you can read my mind. I am always ready for snack time."

"We'll have snack after morning meeting," said Ms. Twohey.

"That is not earlier than normal."

"Oh, you."

Bax was sitting next to Stewart, talking intensely. The dogs sat at the desk on the other side of Stewart. Stewart nodded at Bax and then leaned over to whisper to the dogs.

"I made a decision. I'm going to quit Junior Office Supply Enthusiasts."

"Stewart, you are doing a thing to make you happy! Are you sure? We want you to be happy."

"Yeah, I'm sure. Office supplies are okay, but your club sounds much more fun."

"You're silly! We're not in a club. What did your parents say?"

"I haven't told them yet."

CHAPTER FIFTEEN

A re you quitting your club because you realized it made you smell bored?" asked Waldo at home that night. "Hey, maybe you can come to our fun hour-long daily playdate!"

"Mostly it was that everyone really loved office supplies," said Stewart. "And forms. I had to go talk to Mr. Nehi today and fill out three Resignation from Club forms."

"Wasn't that the point of the whole club?" asked Sassy. "Pencils and paperwork?"

"Well, yeah," said Stewart. "And I realized I don't love office supplies as much as everyone else. Don't get me wrong. Office supplies are great. But am I an enthusiast? No. They kept asking me for my input on the float and I kept thinking about other things."

"Like what?"

"Like how I'd rather be playing with both of you."

"You are the best boy!" said Sassy.

"We are so happy!" said Waldo.

"The Rover Scout float is going to be so great," said Stewart.

"Whatever that is," said Waldo.

"So how are you going to tell your parents?" said Sassy. "Maybe you can just tell them about how Mr. Nehi organizes tape dispensers? They would like to hear about that."

"Yeah, probably," said Stewart. "That's what I'm worried about. They're so into office supplies, and I don't know if they'll be happy to hear that I don't like pencils as much as they do."

"But you like pencils a little bit, so it will all be okay," said Waldo.

"You should first write them a note," said Sassy. "I have learned from Ms. Twohey that if you are having trouble saying something, you can write it down."

"Like that time that I had to write a note explaining how we ate everyone's lunch by mistake," said Waldo. "That was easier to write down instead of saying out loud."

"Maybe I will write them a note telling them I need to talk to them," said Stewart. "If I tell them about switching clubs in a note, they will get distracted by which paper and pen I use and might not actually read the words."

"You will write them a note and I will help," said Waldo.

"First I will nap," said Sassy.

"Also I will nap," said Waldo.

"Do you want to nap while I write the note?" said Stewart.

"Yes!" said both dogs together.

So Stewart wrote his parents a note saying he had something to tell them, and then he woke the dogs and they all went to the living room.

"You can do it," said Sassy.

Stewart's parents came into the living room and sat on the couch.

"What's this about, son?" said Stewart's dad. "Your note made it sound serious. Plus you used blue paper, which is a serious paper."

"I do like how you used different pen colors," said Stewart's mom. "And how you made a smiley face out of staples."

"Mom," said Stewart. "Dad."

"Yes?" said his parents.

"I have decided something."

"Yes?" said his parents.

"I am switching clubs."

"Oh boy!" said Stewart's dad. "Are you moving up to Junior Senior Office Supply Enthusiasts already?"

"No, I'm going to be a Rover Scout."

His parents just stared at him, confused.

"Rover Scouts is this cool new club that's all about exploring and, uh, sports. And food preparation," said Stewart.

"A *new* club?" said Stewart's dad. "Well, I don't know."

"Don't you see, dear?" said Stewart's mom. "He'll be getting in on the ground floor. He'll be one of the *founding members*. One hundred years from now schoolchildren will wear pins with Stewart's face on them!"

"Uh . . ." said Stewart.

"Do you think someone will write a musical about him?" asked Stewart's dad.

"Probably!" said Stewart's mom.

"But still. How could you give up office supplies?" said his dad.

"They still use office supplies in Rover Scouts, Dad. And it will be real-world office supply experience. I won't just be talking about office supplies, I'll be using them."

"You know what, Walter? I just got a great idea!" said Stewart's mom.

Stewart's dad quickly pulled a small spiral-bound memo pad and a pen out of his pocket. "I love when you get ideas! Write it down!"

"We should have our own Office Supply Enthusiasts meeting, right here in our own home!"

Stewart's dad jumped up and ran to the coat closet in the hall.

"Let's start right now!" he said. "We have everything we need!"

The inside of the closet had shelf after shelf of neatly organized office supplies. The parents started squealing with glee.

"Well," said Stewart, who was still in the living room with the dogs, "I guess that went okay, huh, guys?"

Both dogs had fallen asleep again.

CHAPTER SIXTEEN

SCHO
DANC

We have the best playtime today!" said Waldo to the Rover Scouts. "We have a human! It's Stewart! Everything is okay now because Stewart is here."

"What about us?" said Charlie.

"You are also here," said Waldo.

"Right, but you weren't this excited when we showed up," said Susan.

"I am very excited for all of you. You are all the best. It's just that Stewart is the best."

"Technically, that makes no sense," said Ralph.

"I brought **cookies**," said Piper.

"You WHAT?" said Waldo. "Piper is the winner!"

"Hey, I brought **popcorn** once," said Bax.

"**Popcorn** is not **cookies**," said Waldo.

"It's better," said Bax.

"Do they make **popcorn cookies**?" whispered Sassy.

"Everyone eat **cookies**!" said Waldo. "And then we will play a game called 'What is a float?'"

"Why?" said Stewart.

"Because I do not know what a float is, except for the kind with **ice cream**. And I have learned that a club can be something besides a **sandwich**. Ms. Twohey taught me about context clues, and I am context cluing to know that we are talking about floats but we are not talking about **ice cream**."

"Okay, everyone," said Stewart. "Salty is from Liver, and—"

"**Liver, Ohio!**" said Waldo.

"Salty is from Liver, *Ohio*," Stewart continued, "and they don't have parades or floats or town holidays there. So we need to explain what a float is."

"Technically, a float is just a pageant on the back of a truck," said Ralph.

"It usually has a theme," said Charlie.

"Sometimes the people on the float throw things into the crowd," said Piper.

"There can be singing and dancing," said Susan.

"Sometimes it's just Mayor Pennywhistle in a car waving at people," said Bax.

"No, that's not a float," said Ralph. "That's the mayor's car."

"Yeah, okay, sure," said Bax. "But if you put the mayor in a car on the back of a truck, then it would be a float."

"Technically, yes," said Ralph.

"Okay, so we will put a car and dancing and a pageant on a truck, and throw something at people," said Waldo. "Easy. Which one of you has a truck?"

"School clubs don't have truck floats," said Piper. "We have a mini float. Which is the size of a truck float, but we'll have to drag it down the street ourselves."

"Maybe we should all stand there saluting, in our Rover Scouts uniforms?" said Charlie.

"We don't have uniforms," said Ralph.

"We could run in circles," said Piper.

"Yes, we're good at that," said Bax.

"You could bounce a kickball," said Piper.

"I might need more than one kickball," said Bax. "Or some of us will have to run into the crowd to get the balls back, if they bounce off the float."

"What if we gather a bunch of tennis balls that have bounced out of the tennis court? Then we don't have to find stray kickballs anywhere," said Charlie.

"This is good," said Waldo. "Our theme is balls! And running in circles!"

"I'm not sure that's a theme," said Stewart.

"Our theme is also food!" said Waldo.

"Huh," said Stewart.

"This is going to be such a great float," said Waldo, sighing, as Sassy slowly lowered herself down to the grass for a nap.

CHAPTER SEVENTEEN

That night at home, there was no dinner. Stewart's parents were so excited about holding another meeting of their in-home, two-person Office Supply Enthusiasts club that they told Stewart he was in charge of feeding himself.

"This is a great opportunity for you to give us **sandwiches** instead of **kibble** for dinner," said Waldo.

"I don't think that's a good idea," said Stewart. "Dogs aren't really supposed to eat people food."

"We get people food for lunch, so why not have it for every meal?" said Sassy.

"I think when it is lunchtime, it does not count, because we are dressed as a human, so we can only eat human food," said Waldo.

Stewart fed the dogs and poured himself a **bowl of cereal**, which made the dogs happy, because it looked like he was eating a **bowl of kibble** too. They ate in happy silence for a few minutes, and it occurred to Stewart that there was something he needed to clarify with his dogs.

"You know that thing you do every day after school now?" he said.

"Our daily hour-long playdate?" said Waldo. "Yes. It is fun. Especially now that you're doing it too."

"You know it's a club, right?" said Stewart.

"What's a club?" said Waldo.

"We are getting a **sandwich** now? I thought you said no people food for dinner?" said Sassy.

Stewart explained to the dogs that Bax had told him about this fun new club called Rover Scouts, where they ran in circles, napped, and ate snacks. He told them about how fun Bax had made Rover Scouts sound, and then how Bax had said that Salty had founded the club and was the scout leader.

"That's ridiculous," said Waldo. "Rover Scout is my detective name."

"What kind of **sandwich** are we getting?" asked Sassy.

It took a while, but eventually Stewart made the dogs understand.

"We're getting the surprise club-starting badger for sure," said Waldo.

"I guess sometimes you are in a room looking for snacks and you start a club without meaning to," said Sassy.

Stewart put his bowl in the sink and they all went up to his room. Stewart read a comic book while the dogs drew pictures of what they thought a good float would look like. It was mostly giant **hamburgers**.

"But with great clubs comes great responsibility," said Stewart.

"What does that mean?" asked Waldo.

"I'm not sure, it just seemed like a good thing to say," said Stewart. "I do know that the Rover Scouts club needs to have a float though."

"I think you mean that we need to have the best float," said Sassy.

"I have been thinking about that too," said Waldo. "It is hard because we only just figured out what a float actually is. I did not know it involved driving and dancing."

"That's what being a human is, silly!" said Sassy. "That's what humans do! They drive to get food, and when they get the food, they dance."

"You are right," said Waldo.

"So this float is really nothing more than a celebration of humanity," said Sassy.

"Wow," said Stewart.

"Here is a thing that I think," said Waldo. "I think that we will be able to make the best float. It will just happen one day."

"That's not how the world works," said Stewart.

"It is how we became a student at Bea Arthur Memorial Elementary School," said Sassy. "It is how we started a club. And it is how we found that humongous **roast turkey** one day in November."

"Again, that was our **Thanksgiving turkey**," said Stewart.

"But it just happened one day," said Waldo. "And then I ate it."

"Yeah, you know what? You're right," said Stewart. "That is totally how the world works."

"So it is all set then," said Sassy. "That's a relief."

CHAPTER EIGHTEEN

A re you worried about the float yet?" Stewart asked the dogs on the way to school.

"Why would we be worried?" asked Waldo.

"There's not really much of a plan."

"I think the real key is that we're the best at napping," said Sassy.

"You can't really make a float about napping though?" said Stewart.

"We can and we will!" said Waldo.

Bax came running toward them across the front lawn as they rounded the corner toward Bea Arthur Elementary.

"Hey, so I've done some light spying," said Bax.

"What?" said Stewart.

"You know, just dabbling in a little morning espionage."

"Wow," said Stewart.

"And it looks like a lot of the other clubs are wrapping up their float designs. I've been listening in on some conversations, and I think the other clubs are almost done. So we should spend today's Rover Scouts meeting sneaking around and trying to see what they have. And that way whatever we come up with will be so much better."

"See?" said Waldo. "It sure is a good thing we left it until the very last minute! If we had planned ahead and done all the work on time, our float would just be a mess of random ideas."

"Pretty sure that's what it's going to be anyway," said Stewart, "but it will be interesting. And I'll admit spying on the other floats sounds like more fun than building a float."

And so after school, Waldo broke the news to the Rover Scouts that, instead of talking about their float for another day, or playing lunch line, or running in circles, they would be spying on other clubs.

"You know what I like about Rover Scouts?" said Piper. "How every day is something new, and it's always something I love doing."

"You love spying on clubs to see what their floats are?" said Stewart.

"Apparently, considering how fired up I am right now," said Piper.

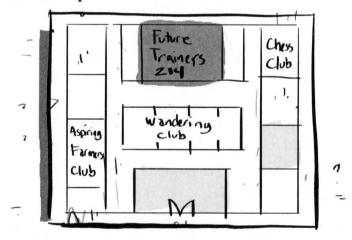

"So I've made a map of the school and where each club meets," said Bax, spreading a map the size of a sprawled-out Labrador retriever onto the grass. "And here"—Bax unrolled several large transparent overlays—"is a minute-by-minute strategy of who should go where, at what time, where they should hide, and what time you need to be done with the operation to avoid detection."

"Whoa," said Charlie.

Bax handed each Rover Scout a small piece of paper. "Your instructions are written in code in disappearing ink. We all need to leave in ninety-three seconds to accomplish our missions in time. Remember: Be observant. Notice details. Make note of anything unusual. And above all: Don't get caught. Is everyone ready?"

"Yes!" said Ralph. "Oh, hang on!" He hopped in the air a few times. He jogged in place. He ran and tried to drop into a somersault, but tripped and fell sideways. "I'm ready now!"

"On your mark," said Bax.

"**On your marble cake**," repeated Waldo.

"Get set," said Bax.

"Get seventeen hams," repeated Waldo.

"Go!" said Bax.

"Go go go!" said Waldo.

The Rover Scouts scattered toward the school, checking their instructions, moving low and swiftly.

Waldo looked at the piece of paper Bax had given him while Sassy zigzagged across the grass in no particular direction.

"This says we should go to room 214 and see what the Future Trainers are doing," said Waldo.

"Who are the Future Trainers?" said Sassy.

"Probably humans who can train the future," said Waldo. "So they all got together and formed a club."

"I want to train the future to rain beef from the sky," said Sassy.

"Get low! Walk quietly!" said Waldo as they entered the school.

Sassy got low. And then she fell asleep.

Waldo poked her with his tail. "Come on! Bax said we have to hurry."

"I'm tired."

"You can do it. We're almost to the room. Let's slink."

Sassy slithered across the cool tiles of the hallway. When Sassy slithered, she became invisible. It was a magic trick she knew. She'd never tested it to make absolutely sure, but she was pretty sure it worked.

They got to the door of room 214. It was open.

"They don't seem to have any concerns about being spied on," whispered Sassy.

"Shhh," whispered Waldo back.

The dogs pressed against the wall and listened.

"Okay, everyone, look at me," said an authoritative voice. "Good. Wait."

When the dogs heard that voice, they quickly put their coat back on.

"I think they're talking about time machines. Everyone should wait until the time machines are ready," whispered Waldo.

"That makes sense," Sassy whispered back. "Why do you think it smells so much like dogs?"

Waldo thought for a moment. "Dogs probably built the time machines. Dogs are smart like that. I wonder if they can get food from the future."

"Maybe there is future **sausage**."

"In the future, every **sausage** is programmed to become two **sausages**."

"Wouldn't that lead to infinite **sausages** pretty quickly?" said Sassy. "It would be a disaster."

"A delicious disaster."

"What are you doing?" Arden was standing in front of Salty. And behind her stood Buttercup, Pistachio, Tugboat, and Jeffy.

"**Wow!**" said Waldo. "**Uh, hi, Arden! Um, wow!**"

"What, you've never seen a dog before?" said Arden.

"Ha ha ha, I, wow!" said Waldo. He wasn't making much sense.

Pistachio barked. She was laughing. The other dogs joined in.

"Easy," said Arden, turning toward the dogs and holding up a treat. "No bark."

But the sight of Waldo and Sassy pretending to be a human student was too much.

"You look so great!" said Pistachio. "And I cannot believe these humans believe you are also a human!"

"I know, right?" said Waldo.

To the students standing there in the hallway in their lab coats, it sounded like Pistachio was barking more. But it sounded like Waldo was talking. Because sometimes when Waldo had been talking human all day, he forgot to switch to dog.

"You know right about what?" said Arden.

"About the time machines and the tennis balls that bounce the squirrels out of the trees. Also what's with all these dogs?"

"That's our club," said Arden. "We're the Future Dog Trainers. We're dog experts. We know everything there is to know about dogs."

At this, Buttercup, Pistachio, Tugboat, and Jeffy burst into uncontrollable laughter. Tugboat rolled over onto his back. Jeffy covered his face with his paws. Pistachio almost peed.

"The most important thing is for the dogs to know that you are in command," said Arden, holding up a treat. The dogs kept laughing but they sat, dutifully, and she gave them each a treat.

"The funny thing," said Tugboat, "is that she doesn't realize how well we have her trained to give us treats every time we bark."

"My person signed us up for parade time," said Pistachio.

"Mine too!" said Buttercup.

"My owner said something about the parade too," said Tugboat. "Something about how she gets five dollars and I get a **biscuit**?"

"Yeah!" said Pistachio. "Yeah! Yeah! That's what my girl said!"

"**Is it hard for you to balance your dog training with your time travel?**" asked Waldo.

"Isn't it time for you to get back to your club, Salty?" asked Arden. "We have important work to do."

The dogs all cracked up again at that.

"Yeah, Salty!" said Buttercup as Waldo and Sassy walked down the hall. "We have important work getting these humans to give us all their **biscuits** and **cookies** and **kibble**!"

CHAPTER NINETEEN

Sassy ran out the door to the back of the school, and straight to a bush so the dogs could collect themselves.

"Do you think she's going to send all our dog friends to the future?" asked Waldo.

"I hope not!" she said.

The dogs tried to figure out if they could sneak in and get the Future Trainers to give them dog treats, but ended up taking a small nap. Running a club was tiring, even if they had been doing it all along without even knowing.

Sassy woke up with a start. "Let's report to the Rover Scouts!"

"That's my detective name!" said Waldo.

Waldo hopped on top of Sassy and they found the rest of their club.

"Bax still isn't here," said Charlie.

"He'll be here soon, I'm sure," said Piper. "He's the one who came up with this whole plan anyway. Salty! What do you know?"

"I know that math is fun and **hot dogs** are nice."

"No, I mean, what did you find out on your spy mission?"

"I have learned that the Future Trainers are going to make a float with time machines and send all the park dogs back to the future."

"Okayyyy," said Piper.

"Are you sure you have all that right?" said Stewart.

"They have dog treats from the future, or maybe from the past, and they are giving them to dogs. What did you find out?"

"I spied on the Aspiring Farmers and they are making a giant sparkling chicken that dances," said Susan.

"The Chess Club is building a huge chessboard on their float, and the people are going to dress as chess pieces," said Stewart.

"I did not know there was a **cheese** club," said Waldo. "Can we join the **cheese** club?"

"I watched the Breakfast Club for a while, but they didn't seem to be doing anything," said Piper.

"There's a BREAKFAST CLUB?" said Waldo. "Was there **bacon** and **pancakes**?"

"There wasn't any food at all," said Piper. "They were just sitting cross-legged in between some book-shelves in the library."

"Hey, guys!" shouted Bax from across the lawn. "Can you give me a hand?"

He was pulling something large behind him. When the Rover Scouts got close, they saw that it was a large wooden platform on wheels, piled high with lumber and plastic piping.

"What is this?" said Stewart.

"It's our float," said Bax. "Or it will be our float. We need to build it still."

"Where did you get all these supplies?" asked Susan.

"From a guy I know."

"You knew a guy who had float supplies all this time and you didn't tell us?" asked Ralph.

"Well, I just met him," said Bax. "I was spying on the Wandering Club and they wandered toward town. I think their float is going to be unfocused wandering."

"On a float?" asked Stewart.

"It seemed like it was going to be floatless wandering," said Bax.

"So technically, they'll just be marching in the parade," said Ralph.

"Keep going with your story," said Piper. "How did you get all this?"

"I was following the Wanderers," said Bax. "I was being the best spy. I hid behind bushes and they never knew I was there."

"So, the float supplies . . ." said Piper.

"Right. So I was sneaking, and we were on this small road behind a bunch of buildings, and there was this guy in a garage with all this stuff. And I thought to

myself, 'Hey, that's all the stuff we need! I'll ask if we can have it!' So I did and he gave it to me."

"He just gave it to you?" asked Ralph.

"Yes," said Bax. "He wants it back after, but I told him that would be no problem."

"**This is good**," said Waldo. "**You did a good job. We are almost done with our float now!**"

"Technically, no," said Ralph.

"Bax got us these supplies because he is a good Rover Scout," said Waldo.

"Yeah, that's right," said Bax. "He didn't want to give them to me at first, but I told him all about Rover Scouts, and how awesome we are, and then I made this face at him."

Bax made his eyes very big. He looked sad, and lonely, and heartbroken, and needy.

"That is very effective!" said Waldo. "I want to give you everything I have!"

"Right on!" said Bax.

"I do not have anything," said Waldo.

"So now all we have to do," said Stewart, "is figure out what to do with all this."

CHAPTER TWENTY

Waldo and Sassy missed the backyard. It had been a rough few days.

The Rover Scouts had spent the last three meetings building their float. There had been a lot of hammering (mostly on the wood but every once in a while someone used a nail) and a lot of painting. Ralph did important work with a glue gun and a tub of glitter.

Piper turned out to have excellent embroidery skills, which were not actually all that helpful. Bax ran around a lot.

Waldo felt like he should know what was going on. But he was still getting used to the fact that they had started a club by accident, and were leading a club by accident, and had discovered the Queen's Refrigerator by accident.

But now they were in the backyard where things made sense again.

"I know that tree!" said Waldo.

"This is a chair I have seen before," said Sassy.

Waldo and Sassy ran in circles like they always did. They were glad to have an after-school club where they could run in circles, but it wasn't exactly the same as their yard.

Stewart lay on his back in the grass. The dogs curled up next to him. The late afternoon sun warmed their faces and soon they were snoring. They woke up a few minutes later when Stewart's mom called to him and told him he had to clean his room.

"Oh, I can't, Mom!" said Stewart, hopping up. "The dogs really need to run! Can't you see how restless they are?"

Sassy yawned.

"They look like they could sleep for hours," said Stewart's mom.

"I promise I'll clean my room later!" said Stewart, poking at the dogs. "We have to go to the dog park!"

Stewart and the dogs ran out and down the sidewalk before Stewart's mom could protest.

"I always wanted dogs," said Stewart, "you know, because dogs are awesome and how you're my best friends and all that. But an added bonus has been that you're a perfect excuse for chore avoidance."

Stewart opened the gate at the dog park, and Sassy and Waldo ran over to greet everyone. Jeffy was standing with the dogs today instead of with the humans.

"Jeffy, you smell like an **oatmeal cookie**!" said Sassy.

"I had a bath," he said.

"I'm sorry."

"It's okay," said Jeffy. "Everyone has to take a bath once in a while."

"I hid under a blanket so I didn't accidentally have to have a bath too!" said Pistachio. "Bath bath bath bath bath!"

"Have you found your home yet, Jeffy?" asked Waldo.

"No," said Jeffy. "Not yet."

"You should ask Arden," said Waldo. "Maybe she can travel to the future and figure out where your home is!"

Jeffy wagged his tail and barked twice.

"Jeffy loves Arden," said Pistachio.

Jeffy wagged harder.

"So we've been to your school, as you know," said Buttercup. "We saw the classroom, which smelled like pencils and books. We saw the hallway, which smelled like dirty sneakers and backpacks. But no one took us to the cafeteria. We did not have lunch. I was led to believe that school means lunch."

"But lunch happens in the middle of the day, not after school," said Waldo.

"Still, I think that if we are going to be school dogs, we should get school lunch," said Buttercup. "Or any lunch."

"I will give you lunch!" said Waldo. "I will give you the lunch you are owed when you are at the parade!"

"You will?" said Sassy.

"I have just figured out that is what we are building on our float," said Waldo. "We can shoot lunch at everyone who doesn't get to have lunch at school!"

"Of course!" said Sassy. "Lunch launchers!"

"You never told us about the lunch launchers," said Tugboat.

"The lunch launchers are something we just made up," said Sassy. "We put lunch into them and then we launch it into the crowd."

"You are heroes," said Buttercup. "And geniuses. And I am very much looking forward to having lunch."

"Do you think Arden will be there?" asked Jeffy.

"Of course she'll be there!" said Tugboat. "We're going to be on her float! She has to be there."

"I didn't know if maybe she stayed home during the parade since she's the star and is so smart," said Jeffy. "Maybe special people like Arden don't go to parades. I don't know."

"She'll be there!" said Pistachio. "Everyone goes to the parade! Float float float float float!"

"If Arden will be there, then so will I," said Jeffy.

The dogs all ran in more big circles, excited by the prospect of being in a parade, until their people told them it was time to go back home.

"We have to go," said Sassy. "Don't forget, everyone, that we will shoot meat at your faces on Saturday."

"ood news!" said Waldo to the Rover Scouts after school the next day. "I have figured out what we are doing!"

"Finally!" said Piper. "The parade is tomorrow!"

"Wait, we don't know what we're doing?" said Susan.

"We did, we just didn't know we knew what we're doing," said Waldo.

"Technically, that's the same as not knowing," said Ralph. "So what are we doing?"

"We are making lunch launchers," said Waldo, and waited for everyone to applaud.

No one applauded.

"What's a lunch launcher?" asked Charlie.

"We are going to shoot lunch at people, from these launchers," said Waldo.

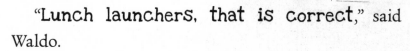

"Now that I look at what we've built, it does look like we're planning on launching something," said Bax.

"Lunch launchers, that is correct," said Waldo.

"Do we have food to launch?" asked Ralph.

"We do not," said Waldo.

"How are we going to launch these things?" asked Ralph. "It's not like we have practiced shooting food from our float."

"With our launchers!" said Waldo.

"But—" said Piper.

"First we have to get the food," said Waldo. "This is our new agenda for today. We are going to play a game called 'Get the Food.' We are all going to go run out now and the person who comes back with the most food wins."

"Does it all have to be launchable food?" asked Piper. "What if I find food that won't fit in our launchers? What if I find a **roast ham**?"

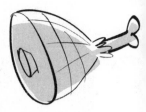

"If you find a **roast ham**, bring it back here first and then go look for more food," said Waldo.

"Wait, so we're just going to go find food somewhere?" asked Susan. "Right now? Where should we look? Our kitchens at home?"

"That is good, yes," said Waldo. Waldo thought for a moment. He liked getting jobs from humans, not being the one who handed out the jobs. "Just . . . just find food! Use your skills! This is what we've practiced for! Sniff it out! Beg! Throw tennis balls at a bear and steal her picnic basket! Meet me back here in five!"

"Five what?" said Ralph.

"That is an human expression that means 'When you have five hundred food items that we can launch during a parade.'"

The Rover Scouts all ran off in different directions. Waldo felt like if anything, he was good at motivating the Rover Scouts. He was proud to learn that he was just as good a motivational speaker as he had always suspected.

"Come on, Sassy," said Waldo. "Let's get food from the Queen's Refrigerator."

Sassy walked toward the school, where they saw Arden sitting on the ground, throwing a tennis ball against the wall. She smelled tired and a little sad.

"Hi, Arden!" said Waldo. "How is the future?"

"That's a weird question," said Arden, catching the tennis ball one last time and putting it in her pocket. "But I don't know how the future is. It all depends on what happens at Founders Day. I have a lot riding on our floats."

"We will all be riding on floats!" said Waldo. "That's what floats are. It's exhausting."

"I know what floats are," said Arden. "I'm just trying to do what's best. Plus you know, my mom will be there, and she'll be watching it all."

"Moms are nice, but sometimes they make you clean your room," said Waldo.

"Yeah. But my mom is the Grand Marshall. Mayor Pennywhistle?"

"Your mom is the mayor and the Grunge Marshmallow? You are Arfen Whistlepens?"

"Something like that. My mom will be watching, so I have to win."

"We all have to win," said Waldo.

"It's all up to the dogs," said Arden. "That part is a bit of a wild card."

"**They are not wild dogs!**" said Waldo.

"I know that," said Arden. "I love dogs. I know everything about dogs. No one knows more about dogs than me."

Waldo looked at Arden for a few minutes. Sassy had fallen asleep, and Waldo adjusted the trench coat so it covered her tail.

"**I know a thing or two about dogs,**" said Waldo.

"Oh, really?" said Arden, raising an eyebrow. "Did you know that dogs have a really strong sense of smell? Did you know that people who have dogs live longer than the ones who don't? Did you know that some dogs can run faster than a lion? Did you know that dogs can't eat **chocolate**?"

Waldo knew all those things. But he could also smell insecurity on Arden, and he wanted to make her feel better. "**You are really smart about dogs. You're right.**"

"I told you."

"**I have to go. We still need to finish up our float. See you around! You're fun!**"

Waldo tapped Sassy's head. Sassy was getting a little annoyed at Waldo always waking her from up there, but mostly she was glad that she got to be the napping half of Salty. The dogs went into the gymnateria.

When they went to slip into the kitchen, they were surprised to find cafeteria workers preparing food.

"Oh, hello, human lunch makers!" said Waldo. "You are my favorite!"

"Hey, Salty, what are you doing back here?" said a lunch lady named Mary Lou.

"Collecting launchers?" said Waldo.

"That must be a new one," said Mary Lou. "Pet sticks, giggle glasses, fidget fliers—I can't keep up with all the trends."

"If you just let me into the refrigerator I will be gone in a spiffy," said Waldo.

"You are a hoot! I can't let you in there, silly."

"Why not?"

"Because you're not a cafeteria worker."

"Could I be?"

"Sure, when you grow up! You'd be a great cafeteria worker. I bet you'd love it as much as I do! Now scoot along, hon, we've got to finish making all these **club sandwiches** for Founders Day tomorrow. We have a lot of work to do. Every **club sandwich** has to be perfect."

"Real **club sandwiches**! Not 'a group of people with a shared interest or goal who meet' **sandwich**?" said Waldo.

"Oh, Salty, such an imagination!"

"Now I know there are **club sandwiches** up there. I can smell them!" whispered Sassy.

"That is a lot of **club sandwiches**," said Waldo.

"You bet. And every one is perfect! Go along now. Good luck catching all your launchers!"

"Did you see all those perfect **club sandwiches**?" Waldo asked Sassy when they got outside.

"Did I ever."

Sassy sat on the blacktop behind the school. The dogs sighed. Something smelled **sandwichy**. And **clubby**. **Clubby sandwichy**, even. Maybe there had been so many perfect **club sandwiches** in the kitchen that the **club sandwich** smell molecules had implanted in their nostrils, and they would smell **club sandwiches** everywhere for the rest of their lives.

Which would be delightful, but also infuriating. It would be a hard life to smell **club sandwiches** but not have **club sandwiches** to eat. Sassy had a hard enough time hearing about **club sandwiches** and never getting to eat one. But to smell them too. That was unbearable.

All they knew was that something smelled like a big pile of **club sandwiches**.

There was, in fact, a big pile of **club sandwiches**. There were hundreds of **club sandwiches** stacked up against a dumpster behind the school.

"That is a pile the size of a bullmastiff!" said Waldo. "Are they for the founders? Will they come get these piles of **club sandwiches** for tomorrow? Humans don't usually pile their food on the ground though."

Sassy looked carefully at the piles of food. "I think," she said, "that these are the not-perfect **club sandwiches**. The filling is falling out of some of them. Lots have too much **mayonnaise**. And look at all those with rips in the **bread**."

"But I think a **sandwich** with rips and messy filling and too much **mayonnaise** sounds perfect," said Waldo.

"I think the founders are pickier than we are."

"What is the rule again? If it's near a dumpster, it must be garbage?"

"That is absolutely the rule."

"How do we get these mastiff-sized piles of **club sandwiches** over to the float?"

"Okay, Waldo, that's all I can stand and I can stand no more. Every day I hear you talking about **club sandwiches** and **root beer floats** and **casseroles** outside the coat and I never get to eat any of them. And now here they are and I'm going to eat them all." Sassy put two **club sandwiches** in her mouth.

"I want to eat **club sandwiches**, but I also want to win," said Waldo, grabbing a **club sandwich** with his mouth.

"That sounds delicious and inefficient," said Sassy while chewing.

"Maybe if we only eat a few, we can do both?"

"Maybe we could get Stewart to help us, because here he comes either with a wheelbarrow or a surprise bath on wheels. I really hope it's a wheelbarrow," said Sassy while grabbing another **club sandwich**.

"Hey! Stewart!" yelled Waldo. "Is that wheelbarrow for these nearly perfect **club sandwiches**?"

"Nope," said Stewart, wheeling it over to Salty. "It's for these office supplies."

ffice supplies?!" said Waldo, peering into the wheelbarrow full of binder clips and rubber bands. "Are you abandoning us for your old club? I thought you liked us!"

"I'm still a Rover Scout to the end," said Stewart. "These are for the lunch launchers."

"Those aren't food," said Sassy. "At least I don't think they are." She lifted her **club-sandwich-crumb**-covered head up from a **sandwich** pile and sniffed. "Nope, not food."

"No, I thought we could use the rubber bands like a slingshot to shoot the stuff through."

"I don't know what any of that means, but can you go dump all that by the float so you have more room for all these **sandwiches**?" asked Waldo.

Stewart emptied the wheelbarrow and then he and the dogs filled it with as many **sandwiches** as they could. It took four trips, but they got them all to the float. And one more into  Waldo's belly, and three into Sassy's.

"**We have found a mastiff of sandwiches**," said Waldo.

"I got **fresh green beans**," said Piper.

"**Nature's candy!**" said Waldo.

"I did it!" said Ralph, hopping from foot to foot. "I went to the **pizza** place on the corner and made sad eyes and they gave me **pizzas**!"

"The people at the corner market said I could have all this **shredded cheese** that 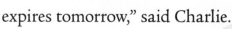 expires tomorrow," said Charlie.

The other Rover Scouts came forward and put their food on the float. There were **french fries**, **donuts**, four foil-wrapped **hamburgers**, a **lemon cake**, nine **enchiladas**, six bags of **potato chips**, two containers of **frozen peas**, and ten pounds of **baby carrots**.

"We are all winners!" said Waldo. "What did you bring, Bax?"

"I got sixteen pounds of **meatballs**, and I just used the materials from this random pile of office supplies I found lying here to make all these slingshot cannons functional."

"BAX WINS," said Waldo.

"Yeah, pretty much," said Ralph.

"Okay, so now we just have to get all this to the parking lot at the municipal gym," said Bax.

"No problem," said Waldo. "We will do it on my count. Twelve! Let's go!"

Ninety minutes later, the sweaty and tired Rover Scouts lined their float up with the others.

"Looking good, team," said Coach, checking things off on a clipboard. "I'm coordinating the Bea Arthur float teams this year. Upload your team music to this digital port. If you need to iron or steam clean any uniforms you can do it over there, and there's a school bespangler over there if any of your sequins need adjusting."

"Thank you for all that helpful information that I'm sure we will not need," said Waldo. "Wow, look at all these floats. Hello, other teams! Your floats are nice!"

"We're Clover Scouts," said a boy dressed in green. "We gather green clovers."

"We're Plover Scouts," said a girl with large, unblinking eyes. "We protect the nesting grounds of the endangered seabird the piping plover."

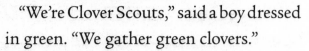

"We're Grover Scouts," said a girl with a bow tie. "We strive to live our lives in the manner of our twenty-second and twenty-fourth president, Grover Cleveland."

"We're Rover Scouts," said Bax. "We run in circles, have snacks, nap, and bounce balls."

"Wow, there sure are a lot of clubs at this school!" said Waldo.

"Sure," said the Plover Scout. "Clubs are important."

"We have to go," said the Grover Scout. "Like Grover Cleveland said, 'Always rest well the night before the big parade.'"

"He said that?" said the Clover Scout.

"Heavens, I don't know. I just like mustaches and bow ties, if we're being honest," said the Grover Scout.

"I think it is very wise," said Waldo. "I haven't napped in one million years, and I need to nap a lot before tomorrow."

"You should have joined Nap Club," said a boy wrapped in a blanket. "It's great." He yawned.

"What's the Nap Club float going to be?" asked Ralph.

"It's that one there," said the boy, pointing at a platform covered in soft pillows. "We're calling it Cozy Wonderland."

"Wow wow wow," said Waldo.

"Hey, Stewart, how's it going in your new club?" asked a girl.

"It's great," said Stewart. "How are the Junior Office Supply Enthusiasts?"

"Oh, we're terrific. We're all very organized." She pointed at a platform with a pile of office supplies in the middle of it. "We are going to do the Dance of the Tape Dispensers."

"Hey, Rover Scouts." It was Arden. "I see you managed to pull something together for tomorrow. Good luck. You'll need it." She waved her arm at the Nap Club's float.

"That is Cozy Wonderland!" said Waldo. "Isn't it amazing?"

"It's okay," said Arden. "Just wait until you see ours." She pointed at a float that had rows of silver plastic flowers hanging down the sides. The top of the float had six low, round platforms about the size of over-turned buckets.

"That doesn't look like much," said Bax.

"Sometimes the simplest floats can be the ones that blow your mind," said Arden.

"I didn't realize the time machines would be so small," said Waldo.

"The what now?" said Arden.

"You know," said Waldo.

"All I'm saying is, our float is the best," said Arden.

"We are all the best!" said Waldo. And he meant it. But the truth was, at the moment, he was the best at being distracted. The floats smelled like glue and paint and wood. The Grover Scouts were eating **hot dogs**.

And on top of it all, there was another smell, which was almost more distracting than the **hot dogs**. Almost. Sassy smelled it too. It was the nervous sweat from all the human students. There were a few who smelled excited, but most of them smelled scared and anxious. The floats were a big project, maybe the biggest project the human students had ever made. Who knew being a human was so much about big projects? That was something the dogs were still learning about.

Sassy walked in a circle for a bit. She was distracted by the nervous smell and also by Cozy Wonderland, so she walked in circles to try to focus. She was just about to focus herself down onto the sidewalk to take a nap when Waldo stuck his head down into the trench coat.

"You know what we have to do tomorrow, right? We have to save all these children from whatever the evil overlord Grunge **Marshmallow** is forcing them to be so miserable about at the Founders Day parade."

"Also we have to throw food at their faces."

"And that."

CHAPTER TWENTY-THREE

The next morning, Waldo and Sassy woke Stewart. They were good alarm-clock dogs. Sassy woke him by licking his face. Waldo woke him by jumping on his chest. It was very effective.

"Today is the day," said Waldo. "We make paradings and also we win, plus we save all the tortured children from the parade."

"Get UP," said Sassy. "We are going to have the most productive day, and I am excited to eat all the **club sandwiches** that accidentally fall out of the lunch cannons."

Stewart's parents made **scrambled eggs**, and even put some **scrambled eggs** on the dogs' **kibble**.

"This day is so great already," Sassy whispered to Waldo.

"I bet you're pretty excited about today," said Stewart's mom. "We'll see you over there. We have to head over early to set up our booth."

"You have a booth?" asked Stewart.

"You bet!" said Stewart's dad. "We're going to see if anyone else wants to join our Office Supply Enthusiasts group. Plus we can just show people how amazing and inspiring office supplies are."

"Why wouldn't they already know that?" said Stewart's mom.

"I know!" said Stewart's dad.

"But we'll see you in the parade," said Stewart's mom. "Good luck!"

Stewart's parents had six tote bags, a rolling case, and a rotating highlighter caddy that Stewart's dad wore like a backpack. They waved and headed out the door.

Stewart and Salty made their way to the start of the parade route. It seemed like everyone in town had turned out for the Founders Day festivities. People lined the streets. Children played carnival games at a midway. The smell of **cotton candy**, **pretzels**, and **deep-fried ice cream sandwiches** filled the air. Stewart had to actively muscle the dogs to the municipal gym parking lot because they kept walking toward the food.

"Hi, guys! You still look hilarious in that outfit!" said Pistachio. Jeffy was behind Arden, following her everywhere she went.

"Thank you! And you all will look hilarious in the future where you are going to be sent from your float," said Sassy.

"The future? I don't want to go to the future, I want to go to the now! Now! Now! Now!" Pistachio scurried away, visibly upset.

"If our dog friends didn't want to go to the future, why did they join the Future Dog Time Machine Club?" Sassy asked Waldo.

Just then Coach blew his whistle and spoke through a megaphone. "Listen up, team! This is your day to shine! I want you to do your best! I want you to bring your A game! I need you to fight through the pain and come out on top! When I say 'HAPPY,' you say what?"

"FOUNDERS DAY!" shouted all the club members.

"HAPPY!" shouted Coach.

"FOUNDERS DAY!"

"HAPPY!"

"FOUNDERS DAY!"

"Do you think this will go on all day?" asked Waldo.

"Seriously," said Arden, who had just walked back next to Salty. "I've got a parade to win."

"Best of luck to you! You're so nice!" said Waldo.

"Uh, okay," said Arden. "Come on, little guy."

Jeffy happily followed Arden to the float, and she picked him up and put him on the platform. She scratched his ears.

"Poor Jeffy. He doesn't even know he's about to be sent to the future where he doesn't know that he doesn't want to go," said Waldo. "So today we have to save the dogs from being sent into the future *and* save the tortured human students *and* win the parade. Today is a lot."

"No problem," said Sassy. "The Future Trainers float is right in front of the Rover Scouts. We can do all these things."

"Technically," said Ralph, when they all got to the float, "we'll need at least eight people to pull the float."

"I want to pull!" said Waldo. Sassy bit his toe. Waldo remembered how Sassy wanted to eat the **club sandwiches** that fell. "I mean, I want to be a lunch launcher."

"I'm totally working a lunch cannon," said Bax.

"Oh, me too!" said Stewart.

There were still plenty of Rover Scouts left over.

And Waldo and Sassy knew just how to fix everything.

"**Rover Scouts meeting! New Founders Day agenda!**" said Waldo. The Rover Scouts huddled around Salty as he explained the plan. Everyone would be using all their best skills, and plus they would save the town and the town's dogs in the process.

"Technically, I don't think the town needs to be saved," said Ralph.

"**It might though**," said Waldo.

"Yeah, okay, that's good enough for me," said Ralph.

CHAPTER TWENTY-FOUR

That's a go, people!" shouted Coach. "On your mark! Go!"

The floats started to lurch slowly out of the parking lot and down Main Street.

The Chess Club was in the lead, trying to position themselves on the rolling chessboard they had constructed.  The club members on the float were all outfitted in giant chess piece costumes, but there was no room in the costumes for their legs to move. The students pulling the float accidentally rolled over a curb, and a rook and a knight fell over and couldn't get back up again.

And none of them, to the dogs' disappointment, were made of **cheese**.

The Junior Office Supply Enthusiasts did an interpretive dance while meaningfully affixing sticky notes to one another.

The Aspiring Farmers were next. Some of them were inside a giant glittery chicken, dancing to a song about farming. Also, they had real chickens, and the rest of the club was working to keep the chickens inside the tiny fence on their float, while also dancing along to the farm song.

The Plover Scouts were dressed as piping plovers and were pretending to fly above a sand dune they had constructed on their float.

The Grover Scouts' float had the words *Once a Man, Twice a President* painted on the side. They were performing a rap about Grover Cleveland that started, "Fiscally conservative, Grover gave 'em goose bumps / Honest and reliable, he impressed the Mugwumps."

Cozy Wonderland was next. The Nap Club did a synchronized stretch-and-yawn routine while lullabies blasted out of speakers.

The Future Trainers, rolling along in front of the Rover Scouts, were clearly planning on shoving dogs into the small time machine buckets and sending them into the future to eat all the future sausage without Waldo and Sassy.

Waldo had to concentrate hard to stay on top of Sassy. The float bumped along the street, stopping and starting suddenly.

Bax loaded a **sandwich** into a slingshot cannon, pulled back on the rubber band, and let it fly. The **sandwich** flew in a satisfying arc toward Mr. Nehi, who caught the **sandwich** in his hand, took a bite, and gave a thumbs-up.

The Clover Scouts were behind the Rover Scouts and had created a meadow on their float. They moved in unison, looking for clovers.

As the floats continued on, Sassy and Waldo could already smell all the human students' worry about not messing up.

"We must save the children!" Sassy shouted. She could shout during the Founders Day parade, and no one would notice. The fact was, Founders Day was loud. "What is happening with all our dog friends? I can't see! Also can you drop me some **ham**?"

Waldo grabbed a **sandwich**, loaded it onto a launcher, and then accidentally ate it before he launched it. He got another **sandwich** and dropped half of it onto the float so Sassy could eat it.

"Heads up, Buttercup!" shouted Waldo, and he launched a huge batch of **meatballs** at the Future Trainers float.

Arden had Jeffy up on his hind legs on one of the buckets, doing an elaborate trick. She was about to reward him with a **biscuit** when the **meatballs** hit.

"Stop sabotaging us!" yelled Arden as all the dogs ate the **meatballs**.

"We want to keep the dogs in the now so they don't get the future **sausage** without us!" Waldo yelled back.

"What?" yelled Arden.

"Who wants **pizza**?" yelled Stewart as he gleefully shot food into the crowd.

"Get ready for **beans**!" shouted Waldo, and he shot **green beans** at the dogs on the float in front of him, or he tried to, but it was harder than he anticipated to use rubber bands to launch **beans**. Most of them fell onto the float, where Sassy ate them.

"This is working great!" said Bax. "Everyone loves being pelted with lunch!"

"There's still time," Waldo yelled to Sassy. "They haven't sent the dogs into the future yet. They're just walking them in circles and making them sit on those buckets."

After all the **meatballs** were finished, the Future Trainers regained control and were making all the dogs on their float lie down, probably to make them easier to fit into the time machines.

The parade was getting louder. The crowd was cheering. Most of the floats had music. Most of the club members were shouting along with the music.

And while the parade was getting louder, the students working the floats were getting sweatier. And with that sweat smell came an even stronger smell of nervousness.

"All the human children are worried about being killed by the evil overlord Grunge **Marshmallow**!" said Sassy.

"I know!" said Waldo. "But they should not worry. Our plan will save them!"

Waldo launched a **baby carrot** at the back of Ralph's head.

"Technically," said Ralph. "Ow."

"Ralph! It is time for you to alert the other Rover Scouts! It is time to set our plan in motion!" Ralph pulled out an air horn and let off one loud blast. Half the Rover Scouts who had been pulling the float let go and went running in formation up the street. They ran together in a big circle to the front of the parade, looping in front of the Chess Club (where only a pawn and a queen were still standing), around the Junior Office Supply Enthusiasts, and between the Aspiring Farmers and the Plover Scouts.

"Hey!" shouted Piper. "Hey, birds! Look over here!" The Plovers, the giant chicken, and the real chickens all turned toward Piper, and a few of the Rover Scouts held up foil they had taken off the **hamburgers**. The birds were all momentarily confused and mesmerized by the sun shining off the foil. Some other Rover Scouts threw **potato chips** and **peas** onto the floats, and the birds were distracted by the food, pecking and fighting over who got **potato chips**.

"There," said Piper. "That ought to keep them busy."

The parade was still rolling forward, but much more slowly now that the Farmers and Plovers had started arguing over **potato chips**.

Piper heard two air horn blasts from farther down the parade. "Time for Phase Two! Let's go!"

The Rover Scouts ran alongside the floats until they were right in front of the Future Trainers. The Future Trainers were busy getting Tugboat, Pistachio, Buttercup, and Jeffy to lie down and roll over.

From their spying, Piper and Susan knew the tennis balls were stored in a special compartment under the float. The Rover Scouts crouched in front of the Future Trainers float, waiting for the signal.

They heard three air horn blasts from Ralph, and Piper and Susan unlatched the compartment. Hundreds of balls rolled out and all over the street. The parade came screeching to a stop.

"Good work, Scout humans!" they heard Waldo shout. He shot pieces of lemon cake at them.

All the dogs on the Future Trainers float jumped off and started chasing the tennis balls. The Future Trainers waved dog biscuits in the air and shouted, "Stay! Stay!" The Rover Scouts abandoned their float and swarmed the Future Trainers float, grabbing the time machines, which really did look a lot like buckets. Still. Better safe than sorry. They had to make sure none of their dog friends got sent to the future.

"Phew," said Bax. "We saved the world. Again."

"Hey!" shouted Arden. "What are you doing? Why did you steal our dog pedestals?"

"So **you could not send them to the future!**" said Waldo.

"What are you talking about?" said Arden. "We're not sending anyone to the future. We want to be dog trainers in the future. That's why we're called Future Dog Trainers."

"And you are going to get to the future in your bucket-shaped time machines!" said Waldo.

"Those *are* buckets," said Arden.

"And time machines!"

"No."

"But how are you going to get to the future, if not in time machines?" asked Waldo.

"We're going to get there the regular way," said Arden. "By living every day until we get there."

Pistachio, Buttercup, and Tugboat came running back to the float. They had bits of **pizza** and **meatball** stuck in their fur. Tugboat had three tennis balls in his mouth.

"Hey!" said Pistachio. "Have you seen Jeffy? He ran off when the tennis balls exploded."

Arden saw the three dogs. She looked around desperately for a moment, and her eyes started to fill with tears. Then she took a deep breath and whistled. It was a loud whistle, almost as loud as the air horn. Well, no, not that loud, but it definitely took all the dogs by surprise.

"JEFFY!" shouted Arden, and everyone turned to see the terrier running through the crowd toward Arden. "Oh, thank goodness you're safe!" Arden crouched down and took Jeffy in her arms, and Jeffy kissed Arden's cheeks.

"I think Arden loves Jeffy too," said Waldo.

They heard five blasts on the air horn. No one knew what five blasts meant. Also they had carried out the whole plan, so they weren't sure what they were supposed to do now.

Ralph came running. "The mayor is coming!" he yelled. "And technically, she looks mad!"

"Uh-oh," said Arden, hugging Jeffy tightly in her arms. He gave her an encouraging lick on the nose.

"We will save you from the Grunge Marshmallow," said Waldo.

A tall lady in a bright red suit walked purposefully toward the students.

"Young lady, what do you have to say for yourself?"

"I'm Sorry!" said Waldo. "Did we not launch you a sandwich?"

"She meant me," said Arden.

"Oh," said Waldo.

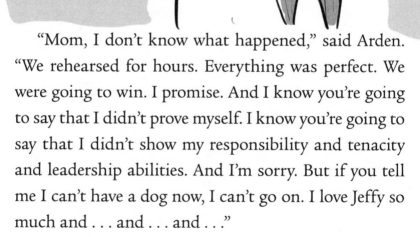

"Mom, I don't know what happened," said Arden. "We rehearsed for hours. Everything was perfect. We were going to win. I promise. And I know you're going to say that I didn't prove myself. I know you're going to say that I didn't show my responsibility and tenacity and leadership abilities. And I'm sorry. But if you tell me I can't have a dog now, I can't go on. I love Jeffy so much and . . . and . . . and . . ."

Arden started to cry.

All the other dogs gathered around her.

"Listen here, Mayor **Marshmallow!**" said Waldo. "Arden is the best dog knower. Except for Stewart. Stewart is really great. But Arden is a human girl who needs a dog! She has been studying so hard and has passed the test and can be a dog trainer in the future and a dog owner in the now."

"Thank you, Salty," said Arden.

"Well, I know that," said Mayor Pennywhistle. "Arden is my daughter, so of course she is the best at anything she does. However . . ."

Arden wasn't crying anymore, but she smelled worried. Jeffy snuggled his nose into her neck. The other dogs all watched Mayor Pennywhistle, who was an alpha human if ever there was one. They couldn't look away.

"However," Mayor Pennywhistle continued, "today's parade has been a disaster. Food was flying. Giant birds were fighting. And I have no idea how we'll ever clean up all these tennis balls. There has never been a Founders Day quite this chaotic."

Jeffy yipped.

"Mommy, I really want this dog. He's my best friend," said Arden.

"Well," said the mayor.

"Grover Cleveland said, 'A day without a dog is a sad day indeed,'" said one of the Grover Scouts.

"Did he now?" said the mayor.

"I have no idea," said the Grover Scout.

"I have seen Arden around dogs," said Stewart. "She's great. Plus poor little Jeffy needs a home."

"I see," said the mayor.

"It's true," said Arden, nodding. "He needs me. Plus you always said if I was going to grow up to be a mayor, I needed to practice. Jeffy can be my first townsperson!"

"He's a dog," said the mayor.

"Dogs are people too!" said Waldo.

"Well," said the mayor. "Oh, fine. As long as you train him not to chase **meatballs** or to cause further Founders Day chaos."

"Impossible!" said Buttercup, but nobody heard her, because they were all cheering.

"Yay!" said Pistachio. "Yay yay yay yay yay!"

"It sure is nice when a dog finds the right person," said Waldo.

"And it sure is nice when a person finds the right dogs," said Stewart.

Coach walked up, blowing his whistle. "Teams! You have to clear your floats from the thoroughfare before you go to the festivities."

"I'm tired!" said Bax, eating a **sandwich**. "I want to nap under a tree and then eat an **ice cream cone**."

"Me too!" shouted the rest of the children.

"Oh, well!" said the mayor. "I guess that wraps up this year's Founders Day parade. Be sure to visit the carnival, the dunking booth, and the reenactment of the founding of our town. And don't forget to stop by the judge's booth to pick up your prize!"

Stewart and Salty got **hot dogs**. They rode on the roller coaster and the carousel. Salty won a prize for Stewart at the carnival, Arden

bought Jeffy a little sweater, and they visited Stewart's parents, who had not managed to convince anyone else to join their club.

"But we don't mind!" said Stewart's mom. "Two is a club!"

Stewart and Salty stopped by the judge's booth, where they each received a blue ribbon.

"We won!" said Waldo. "We got the winner ribbon! Wait, the Clover Scouts have the same winner ribbon. Why is that?"

"Everyone gets a ribbon," said Stewart.

"So who won?" asked Waldo.

"I guess we all did?" said Stewart.

"What great news!" said Waldo. "Congratulations to you! And also you over there! We are all winners! Though Stewart is the best, but I'm sure you already knew that."

Sassy looked out from inside the coat with a **club sandwich** in each paw. "I am also the winner!" she said.

Stewart and the dogs sat down in the grass. Founders Day had been a lot. But it had been great. They'd saved the children from the Grunge **Marshmallow**, and stopped the dogs from being sent to the future. It sure was fun to run a club. Even if you didn't realize you were doing it. Maybe especially then.

"Stewart," said Sassy. "Next time we don't know we're doing something, we'll be sure to tell you."

Julie Falatko writes quirky books about misunderstood characters trying to find their place in the world. She is the author of *Snappsy the Alligator (Did Not Ask to Be in This Book)*, which was published to four starred reviews and coverage in the *New York Times* and *People*. She is also the author of *Snappsy the Alligator and His Best Friend Forever (Probably)* and *No Boring Stories*, as well as many more forthcoming books. To learn more about Julie, please visit juliefalatko.com.

Colin Jack is the illustrator of a number of books for children including *If You Happen to Have a Dinosaur, Under-the-Bed Fred, 1 Zany Zoo*, and the Galaxy Zack series. He also works as a story artist and character designer in the animation industry and has been involved in the production of *Hotel Transylvania, The Book of Life, The Boss Baby*, and *Captain Underpants: The First Epic Movie*. Born in Vancouver, Colin currently resides in California with his wife and two sons.